A Cold Hard

TRUTH

A Cold Hard
TRUTH

Eric Pete

E-FECT PUBLISHING

A Cold Hard Truth

Published in the United States by E-fect Publishing, 2016.

ISBN 13: 978-0-9704995-3-0

ISBN 10: 0-9704995-3-1

E-FECT PUBLISHING

PO Box 2262 Spring, TX 77383

Dedication

In memory of Edna Mae.

And many, many thanks to Marsha, my rock.

Oh. And for the readers...

Ready for some fun?

Let's do this.

Can't stop. Won't stop. Believe that. – Eric

1-Last Year

The Middle East-Location Classified

PLUMES OF BLACK SMOKE rose up to the sky like fingers toward Heaven. The black helicopter flew in low over the rioting masses and random fires, two gunners hanging out the side alert for trouble below. A rocket propelled grenade was not uncommon in this area code, so they kept their eyes trained on the rooftops and ornate minarets of the Old City. Ten miles further inland, it arrived at a walled palace where it hovered overhead for several minutes, awaiting further instructions. Once it received clearance, it landed on the grounds and unloaded its crew of heavily armed professionals. An explosion in the distance momentarily gave them pause, but it was too far away to pose a threat.

"Sideshow, we've arrived at the compound. I repeat, we've arrived. Over," the lead man in nondescript camouflage said into his radio as he signaled with his hands for his men to fan out on their trek toward the looming stone security wall.

"Roger that, Cotton Candy," the voice coordinating this mission from half a continent away replied. "Sheikh Al-Bin Sada and his entourage may have flown the coop, but we still show three heat signatures on the ground. Also, the rebels are advancing from town about a click to the east. Gonna get hairy if they find any non-believers."

"Don't get your knickers in a twist. We ain't gonna be long. Out," the field team leader ended as the group of seven sped up their pace, entering the compound with their short barrel rifles at the ready. Contrary to how they looked, they weren't here to rescue or stage an assault. This team was merely scavengers in search of valuable scraps left behind in the wake of the sudden overthrow and total chaos that had engulfed the tiny, but wealthy country. Maybe they'd find treasure. Maybe it was valuable intel on neighboring countries or passcodes to anonymous bank accounts. Perhaps it was something as innocuous as family photos or lists of names.

There was money to be made or power to be cultivated from this endeavor. No matter the findings, they were simply tasked to gather it up, get out before whatever passed as legitimate authorities came upon them and let those funding this mission sort it all out.

It took three quick kill shots to dispatch the two frightened guards left behind. The group pressed on, leaving one of their own to cover their six near the main entrance while the rest split up to cover the most territory. Inside, the team went through strewn papers and peered behind priceless works of art while leery of potential booby-traps. The Sheikh's departure was so hasty that a music video hailing the country's World Cup team still played on loop over the surround- sound system until abruptly halted by their machine gun fire. Coming upon an unlocked iron door, the team huddled up, their battle-hardened senses on edge, as they prepared for the darkness of the great unknown below. But not before popping a flash-bang grenade and letting it roll down the stairs first.

The explosion was more sound than fury, but whoever was on the receiving end would be debilitated. Goggles on, the team lurched single file down the steps, each aiming at a different sector. Once they adjusted to the dim light and clearing smoke, they removed their goggles and continued on, cautiously approaching a line of rusted bars. Six holding cells reeked of feces and sweat, daring them to hurl as each walked past. The burly man in the lead abruptly signaled for the team to halt as he heard faint breathing coming from the fourth cell on his left.

"Sideshow, we got a warm body. Over," he radioed upon the discovery. The soldier trailing him fired a single shot at the cell door, shredding the lock. Two more swiftly entered to assess the situation.

"Come again? I say, 'repeat'," the command center asked, a bit of nerves creeping into the voice.

"Housekeepers are all accounted for. But the Sheikh has a houseguest he left behind. Over."

"And?" the concerned voice squawked. "What's your assessment, Cotton Candy? Over."

"The bloke's not here of his own free will. Over," he said as the men dragged a frail, bearded houseguest into the center of the square. The field leader fetched a cell phone from his side pocket and aimed it at the haggard face. "He might be a Yank. Uploading image for identification. Over."

Several tense, excruciating minutes passed with the other squad members recommending shooting the man and getting on with their original mission. But their field leader gruffly overruled them, demanding they back off and be patient.

The thin, shivering man heard it all, yet said nothing to his unexpected liberators. He just kept glaring straight ahead as he had all these years. His hate had nourished and sustained him; hate for one man.

The man responsible for his current predicament.

"Cotton Candy, this is Sideshow. We've got a possible hit on your companion. The asset is of value. Do not dispose-I repeat-Do not dispose. Over."

Soon, the newly liberated man thought with the barest hint of a smile, feeling his faith rewarded.

ERIC PETE

2-Joseline Gunn

The Past-Brookline, Massachusetts

It was an overcast day in Boston, ready to turn even bleaker for some. I parked my rental car mere blocks away then merged with the foot traffic destined for Beacon Street and the Green Line "C" Branch light rail. I presented myself like a banker in my new Armani pantsuit with accessorized briefcase, but I was more into contracts and terminations.

More specifically, I had a contract to terminate Vasili Orlovsky, brother of local Russian Mafiya head Leonid Orlovsky. It was one hundred thousand up front and another hundred upon completion of the job. This was to be my final meeting when Leonid would give me the best place to say "do svidaniya" to his not so dear brother.

I'd been freelancing under the radar since leaving the Nest, a society of female killers who were the best at what they do and ain't shit to fuck with. But I was never one for too much formality and their wannabe Amazon code had worn thin as I grew into womanhood. I knew I could never go back, but their skills and training were with me forever. A few more of these jobs and maybe I could lead a normal life, maybe even buy a puppy.

"Excuse me, Miss," a balding middle-aged brother in a trench coat and sunglasses offered, gently tapping me on my shoulder. I don't quite know how he was able to sneak up on me. My former sisters back at the Nest would laugh at me for being so sloppy. And his wearing sunglasses in this overcast weather was alarming. "Detective Jackson, Boston PD. Can I have just a moment of your time?" he added as he flashed a badge. No wonder he was able to sneak up. He was expecting me.

"I'm running late for work, Detective. And really can't miss this train," I admonished with a bit of a fake smile. *Joseline, what the fuck have you gotten yourself into?* I thought silently as my muscles tensed. I scanned the disinterested faces of passengers scooting around us, wondering if any were his backup.

I considered how best to kill him just as he matter-of-factly uttered, "Oh. Before you think about doing what comes naturally, I've got two snipers trained on you. Whatever's in your briefcase or that hidden ankle holster can wait until you hear me out. I just want to talk. Really. And I'll even pay for your time."

Pay? Now he was speaking my language. I was running way ahead of schedule anyway, so decided to go along with the program for now. Perhaps he was a dirty cop hired by one of the Orlovsky Brothers to test me. "I don't know what I can help you with, but you're the law, so lead on."

"I know better than that. I insist. After you," he suggested instead, motioning me to walk ahead.

He picked the nearby Odessa Diner situated next to a crowded Dunkin Donuts, somewhere pretty non-threatening I supposed. As soon as we sat in a window booth, the waitress greeted us in her own homey way, dropping her Rs like the Southies due east of here. The Detective ordered two cups of coffee and a single slice of pie for the both of us. I hated pie, but kept my smile. I could always stab him with the extra fork if it came down to it. Getting a closer look at his features, I noticed traces of applied makeup around the edges of his face and nose. He was wearing a disguise and was no cop. Probably wasn't bald either.

"Don't think I have to pull a gun on you to leave a lasting impression. Because I can relieve you of an eyeball with this soup spoon anytime I feel like it," I snarled from behind clenched teeth as soon as the sweet waitress waddled away.

"Where did you train? One of those schools in Europe? The Caribbean? The women are always the deadliest," he rattled off, trying to keep me off guard as he pretended to further review the menu. His way of watching without watching made me uneasy.

"You said you'd pay me. Right?" I reminded him, already tired of whatever little game he was playing. And that talk of snipers outside was probably bullshit too.

"My currency is information. Information that's gonna save your life. By now you know I'm not really a cop."

"Of course," I replied as I began to select pressure points and kill zones on his body. With no money on the table, this waste of time was coming quickly to an end. "But how did you know to stop me at the train?" I questioned, curious whether any more trouble was to come.

"You've got the look while trying not to look it," he answered before letting a chuckle escape. I honestly have never seen anyone so at ease in front of someone like me. "Okay. I made an educated guess," he admitted with a shrug. "Y'see. I had a job to do too....and a target as well."

"I'm warning you. I will put a bullet through your fucking skull and not lose any sleep," I threatened.

"Relax. I'm not your competition. And someone as pretty as you certainly isn't my target. I'm just doing you a favor. You don't want to go to that meeting with your boy Leonid."

"Why not?" I scoffed. "I can handle his brother Vasili plus his crew."

"But what if it's *both* crews-Vasili and Leonid? An ambush," he spelled out for me.

"That doesn't make sense. Because Leonid—"

"Hired you to take out his brother," he spouted, cutting me off. "I know because Vasili hired me to do the same thing."

"So why the double-cross? You have no honor," I spat, my beloved Nest conditioning asserting itself.

"No. Honor is for the sentimental and foolish. But the only double-cross is the one they're trying to pull with us. Even if you don't believe it, I just saved your life. Feel free to thank me at any time."

Our waitress returned with our coffee and pie, making me pause for a moment.

"Thank you?" I scoffed before she'd barely taken a step away. "Spit it out before I ventilate you on sheer principle."

"It's just this simple. Our little Russians made up. Mended fences just like their momma would want and screwed me out of my money in the process. Vasili and Leonid want to put on a united front for the other families on the East Coast. Need to eliminate any appearance of them having been at each other's throat."

"Bullshit."

"What was 'bullshit' was them hiring us for our skin color. A really poor moment in affirmative action history," he dryly joked as he slid the corner of his fork into the pie, proving it wasn't poisoned. "I was hired to deal with Leonid in my own way. But Leonid was more direct with how he wanted his brother Vasili handled; hence, you and your particular set of skills. Both picked us for the melanin in our skin. Can't say the Brothers Orlovsky don't think alike. It's plausible deniability for both of them if some *chorns* make a move instead. They could always blame on it on the Jamaicans or Haitians or something."

"You're fuckin' lying," I hissed, stifling a gasp.

"Oh I do lie and I do it very well. Just not now."

"Those fuckin' racists," I cursed, ready to swear up and down in Spanish like my dear Dominican grandmother up in Heaven.

"They're career criminals of the highest order. Did you expect something more out of them? They got chatty over vodka at my last meeting and I understand enough Russian to put it all together. Idiots actually believed I was deaf. Look, they've already screwed me out of my funds because they decided to patch things up. Now they plan on getting their money back from you before...," he paused, letting me paint my own picture with regards to their final intentions. I'd seen Leonid's men and the way they leered at me.

"They'll get more than that. A hell of a lot more," I vowed, eager to remove more than their lusty smiles.

"I don't doubt it. I'd make them pay for their miscalculation. Oh. Here's a detailed layout of the warehouse where you're supposed to have your little meeting," he offered, handing me a sketch he'd made on a diner napkin in just the short time we'd been talking.

"And what do you get out of it?"

"Revenge. Duh," the egotistical prick replied. I kinda liked the brother's cockiness, but he was creeping toward insufferable.

"Wanna help me with the get-back?" I threw out there, curious as to his skills. Wanted to see what he looked like beneath that makeup...and those clothes too. He was definitely younger than he appeared. And far more fit by his posture.

"Nah. I ain't a killer, pretty lady. I'm worse," this chameleon boasted.

"What's worse than putting them in their graves?" I countered, finally smiling. I had a bloodlust that leaving the Nest never really sated.

"Leave Vasili alive for me and perhaps you'll hear about it," he crowed as he took a quick sip of coffee, placed a crumpled twenty dollar bill on the table then darted out the cafe.

ERIC PETE

3- *Truth North* (*You don't want to know him*)

"I don't like this," I grumbled into the earbud mic as I glared at my phone's screen. Humbly adorned in a hoodie and a pair of shorts, I sat at a bus stop while pretending to wait on a bus that was never coming. The streaming image I observed was of Sophia via the webcam I'd hastily set up across the street from her impromptu meeting at a tiny motor-court lodge bordering the Fort Lauderdale Hollywood Airport.

"I know, baby. Because this ain't your job," she reminded me, chirping in her earpiece as she sauntered through the parking lot. As usual, the girl was dressed more for South Beach than South Broward. While she preferred shining bright like a diamond, I felt more at home in the shadows. I'd taken a back seat to most of these jobs in recent years, letting Sophia have her fun instead. I was in a different place these days, I suppose. Discovering you're the father of a preteen you didn't know existed while deep in the middle of a plot to kill her stepfather can do that to you. But that's a story for another day.

"No. Because we're back here," I forcefully corrected her. "You know I've intentionally avoided South Florida since—"

"Since you rescued me from the Sheikh down in Coral Gables," she snapped, cutting me off from my rant about days past.

"And you got me shot for my troubles," I added just for good measure as I popped a fried lobster bite into my mouth from the Styrofoam container resting in my lap. I wasn't gonna play virtual nursemaid to Sophia without some sustenance and the Miami restaurant Finga Licking was the only upside to my return.

"I know. I know. Guilty as charged. And you've done so much to remind me of that," she said as she adjusted her earpiece, inferring a threat to remove it and cut me off. "But don't forget, you've put me through shit too."

That sounded rather ungrateful of her. I'd only removed a malignant cancer from her life by the name of Ivan Dempsey. Sophia suspected my hand in Ivan's mishap and she'd be right...if I ever admitted it, but she had no proof. Dude was nothing more than a manipulative, toxic ex-boyfriend of hers who I used as a solution to my problem at the time. To the general public, Ivan tried to assassinate the Orleans Parish D.A. That same person just so happened to be my daughter's stepfather. Don't worry; the D.A. survived the attempt. Ivan? Well, he lost...permanently. Life can be complicated to say the least, but I was certainly one for out-of-the-box solutions whatever they may be.

"Why do you have to take a job involving rappers?" I pushed, getting back to the here and now of the mission at hand. At some point in the future, I guess the issue of what really happened to Ivan would have to be dealt with, but not now.

"Correction. Singer. Theo Clark is a singer who only sometimes raps. El Jefe Blaque is the rapper," Sophia touted, reminding me of the difference.

Theo Clark and El Jefe Blaque was the newest celebrity feud in the music world. These sensitive dudes on #TeamLightskinned thought they were thugs because their money allowed them to live out their *fantasies on fleek* of orgies, entourages, blunts and broads. But this also made them more prone to overreact at perceived slights, both real and imagined.

"You know what I mean. We've been doing jobs for tech moguls and heads of state. Sophia, this ain't on our level," I tried reminding her. "Why must you insist on lowering your standards?"

"Nigga. Don't try to act brand new," she retorted with a hiss. "You got your start doing dirt for On-Phire Records, so you know you ain't no better. Just because you've lost your taste for the game, don't mean I got to as well. Besides, entertainment is the new royalty. So stop your bitchin' and lemme handle this."

"Okay. Okay. I'll stop. But I don't like you doing this alone and in person. Go-betweens are always safest," I futilely tried to remind her. There was a way of going about these things. "You could've at least worn a disguise or dressed a little less conspicuous."

"I already told you, boy. I do things my way. Besides, I want a selfie with Theo Clark. I got distant cousins that are big fans of his. And unlike you, I like Instagram. How's it gonna look if the people don't know it's me in my own post?"

"Well, at least keep me in your ear," I ordered as a car slowed for the red light in front of me.

"So you can talk dirty to me like you did last night?" she teased. Yeah, we were fucking again. I couldn't help it. Have you seen, Sophia? Exuding raw sex appeal, the former model was no joke. Even a guy with my kind of control has needs and she certainly knew how to fulfill them.

True to form, Sophia ditched her earpiece anyway just to be difficult.

But that wasn't my only way of keeping tabs on her. I'd never let Sophia get in over her head again. Mainly because it was too much of a hassle to come in on the back end and salvage things. Rescuing her last time is what got me noticed by the wrong people. I'm just glad they were no longer around to harm us.

I exited the app I was using and shot off a quick text. While waiting for a reply, I scarfed down another bite of my food then handed off the rest to a homeless passerby who looked hungrier than me. The person on the other end finally hit me back with a simple "K." followed by a link on which I clicked. I knew a hotel like this was the kind to keep tabs on their guests. The kind of tabs the cops would deem illegal if they figured it out. Except I ain't the police, so it didn't take much of a bribe for the underpaid clerk to make me privy to their feed once it was known which room Theo Clark and his crew were in. Sophia had barely been alone in the room with them when the poor video quality allowed me to be a guest as well as long as they didn't take it to the bathroom. As it buffered, there was a lag between what I saw and what they were saying, but I made do.

"Nigga and his boys catfished me last year," Theo Clark admitted to Sophia as I adjusted my earbud to better hear over the traffic noise. "Got me good. But that was only because he was all in his feelings over his thot-ass ho. Flew that bitch down to the 305 and fucked her in the ass. My dawgs know whassup," he asserted. That might've been that Chicago socialite El Jefe Blaque thought he was in love with until he wasn't.

"And you want to pay El Jefe Blaque back for catfishing you...after you fucked his *bitch*?" Sophia asked for clarification while kinda mocking him on the sly.

"Exactly! See, she know what's up!" the bad boy singer yelled gleefully to the three other men of his immediate clique who stood in a loose circle, dapping them up. "It's like you reading my mind, lovely lady."

"I do my best, sweetheart. What kinda services are you looking for, Mr. Clark? How drastic do you wanna go?" Sophia asked.

"Please. Call me '*Tee Cleeeezay*'," he sang in that falsetto of his I'd heard in some of those stripper-filled music videos, probably trying to angle for a whole separate deal with Sophia once this was over.

"Okay, Tee Cleezy," Sophia responded with almost a schoolgirl giggle. "It's your money, so do you have any thoughts on what you want done to El Jefe?"

"Well...*allegedly*, I might want El Jefe fixed up with a tranny. Like one where he can't tell until it's too late. Then BAM!"

"Yeah! Yeah! She need to be one of them *exotical* broads like Rita Ora!" one of Clark's boys lingering out of camera range exclaimed, butchering the English language. "But with a dick!"

"Yeah, like that," Theo agreed. "Exotic, but not really a chick, ya dig?"

"Totally," Sophia replied. "That could certainly be arranged....allegedly."

"But I want him to fall hard for her. Allegedly."

"Hmm. Okay," Sophia grumbled. From her tone, I could tell she was probably rolling her eyes over this cat's teenage revenge fantasy. How much champagne, coke and Molly had these cats snorted and ingested before coming up with this? I might've been ready to hand Clark his money back, but this wasn't my show as she'd already reminded me.

"Then I want her to break his heart all over social media. But I need her to be foreign with no connection to me or my crew whatsoever. No blowback. My label already warned me," he added for clarification.

As I listened and squinted my eyes past the streetlamp glare on my screen, my phone suddenly went dark. I backed out the link then clicked on it again, but still nothing happened as it refused to connect. I held my phone up to check signal strength, but it was perfectly fine. The problem must've been on the hotel's end.

"Shit!" I cursed as I sprang to my feet at the bus stop and began a brisk shuffle down the street. I resorted to my personal video feed of the hotel exterior and parking lot as wild thoughts raced through my head. Absent a gun on me, I began using my most dangerous weapon, my mind, determining what to use or say depending on what I might encounter upon arriving at that dilapidated motel room.

Just as I came into view on the edge of my phone's screen, the side door to the motel flung open. A lone Sophia walked right by me like she'd been taught, only giving me the faintest of smiles in passing. I continued inside like I was just another paying customer, not stopping until my phone rang.

"You were worried?" Sophia asked as I witnessed a motel door open and Theo Clark's men peer out first.

"Nah," was my brief reply as I adjusted my hoodie and turned my back to the hip hop entourage.

"Admit it," she playfully prodded.

"Nah. I was just repositioning myself like any good backup," I lied.

"Uh huh. Well, you can turn back around and meet me at the car. We're done."

"All good?" I asked.

"Yeah. Deal's still on. But I gotta go shopping first."

"Where? Bal Harbour? Aventura?" I questioned, thinking about some local malls that Sophia might want to hit up for retail therapy to celebrate her newest payday.

"No. Europe," she replied.

4-Truth

Atlantic Ocean, 40,000 feet

"We should've flown coach," I said while ironically clinking my champagne glass against hers. The upper level lounge of the Air France A380 knew the two of us as a Chicago car dealer and his pampered wife. At least we got that story straight on the way to the airport.

"Boy, shut your mouth," Sophia shushed me. "This is my job and I don't skimp."

"We could've at least flown out of a different city. We stayed too long in South Florida," I continued, still smiling as I assessed the other first class passengers mingling on the trans-Atlantic flight: Middle Eastern man in bespoke Savile Row suit; roundish, balding neurosurgeon from Indiana; typical indifferent, French couple; tall fashion model type; stoic Scandinavian looking meathead; and Nigerian oil man. All it took was one of them to be hiding behind a fake smile as well.

"Nobody's following us, Truth. Especially on a job like this," she scoffed as she scarfed down some mixed nuts and motioned for another glass of Taittinger Comtes de Champagne. "This is easy money."

"The big time model never changes," I teased while admiring her beauty.

"No. Never 'big time'," she corrected me, a more serious demeanor overcoming her. "I was just a 'model', which don't mean shit in LA if you ain't a household name, on a magazine cover, or dating an A-lister. And back then, we didn't have Instagram 'n shit or reality shows to build our brands. We were just a bunch of pretty people in a pretty town with no time to hear the truth. I was determined though to make my way before I met Ivan and he introduced me to that white girl," she said, referring to that deceased no-good of an ex and their shared cocaine addiction. "I thought we were both chasing the dream, but before I knew it, we were both chasing highs and hustles instead. We were pretty on the outside, but rotten on the inside. Gawd, I'd turned into my momma."

"She was…?" I began.

"A crackhead," Sophia readily answered. "Sold her body until she wound up in prison and I wound up in foster homes."

"I had no idea. I'm so sorry," I gasped.

"Don't be. You ain't had nothing to do with it," she remarked, resting a hand on my arm. "And what about your momma? She was a saint?"

"Mine? She loved me, but loved her dream of fame and being wanted by a man even more. She used to be in that soap opera, *The Edge of Nowhere*. I was a child and we both were damaged goods. Of course, Jason North had a lot to do with it. He was her brother. On the day he had his accident in Monaco, I told him I knew he was my father."

Sophia sat silent, leaving me to think my revelation was too much. To my surprise, she burst out laughing. "Was I believable?" she asked me, a big grin plastered on her face.

"Huh?"

"The shit I made up about my momma. I learned from you. Start with the truth then let the lie fit where it should. So I had you fooled?" she questioned, eagerly sliding in her seat.

"Totally," I replied, kinda impressed.

"My momma wasn't a damn crackhead, boy. She and my daddy ran a tow truck company outta Hawthorne. Boys in my hood used to tell me I was the prettiest girl they ever knew, so I figured might as well do something with it. Now that shit about Jason North being your dad and your momma being in the soaps? Way too out there. Tone it down next time and keep it grounded," she instructed as if imparting some wisdom.

"I just did that to try something different," I said with a smirk, allowing her continued belief my confession was a lie. One of my few times being that honest and it went to waste. Still, Sophia had gotten better with her lies; pride and sadness fought a war inside me over the notion.

The tall, slender woman with the pronounced ass stood up to stretch, seductively shifting her long brown hair aside to expose her neck. I'd seen this move before, but from bedside. The war inside me ended in a hasty truce, both sides ceding the field to a more pleasurable emotion, lust.

"We got eight hours to go and I hear these A380 restrooms are very roomy," she purred as she wiggled a finger for me to follow.

"You have an impressive wife, Mr. Decker," the London educated Pakistani chap chimed as we passed. "You'll have to share your secrets before we get off this flight."

"Oh, I'm not his wife," Sophia replied for me, purring like a kitten. "I'm his naughty little whore. Ain't that right, Big Daddy?"

I just shrugged, leaving the gentleman in stunned amazement as I dealt with the profound tightness in my briefs.

"You're bad," I grinned as we slipped into the bathroom and locked the door behind us. She was right. It was more spacious. Not that it mattered because the space between our bodies was indistinguishable the moment we entered.

"Knew it'd get you all hard," she disclosed, her quickened breath on my face as she stroked me through my pants. "You like this, huh?"

"Yeah," I grunted in reply. "You were right. It is a nice bathroom."

"You got jokes and I'm horny," Sophia commented as she forcefully unbuckled my belt and unzipped my pants. My pants and briefs slid down around my ankles so fast, I felt I was part of a magic show. Aroused as fuck, I reached out to take her in my arms and kiss those juicy, glossed lips.

"Nope. Keep your hands to yourself," she barked as she backed up out of my reach, leaving me to stare at my own hard dick in the mirror. "I'm the one who showed initiative, so I get to reap the benefits."

Keeping her crimson-bottomed heels on, she reached under her designer emerald dress, sliding her black silk panties off those toned golden legs of hers. Then she slowly, seductively slipped her dress off her shoulders, flashing breasts whose pert nipples my mouth yearned to suck. She hoisted her ass and parked it onto the edge of the sink and beckoned me closer. "Bring my dick here and make me cum," she said, biting a fingernail as she parted her legs. As flawless as the pussy looked on the outside, it was equally rewarding for those who got to experience beyond the window dressing. I mean, this girl had a Sheikh holding her captive over it.

I eagerly obeyed and shuffled over to her as she rubbed her clit in tiny circles. Corralling her within my arms, I gripped the sink on both sides of her hips. "Permission to proceed," I requested, playing along.

"Granted," she offered as she threw her head back and slid forward onto me, moaning as she adjusted to my girth inside her moist pussy. I flexed my hips and pumped slowly at first, driving in and out to the roar of the plane.

"Shit, you drive me crazy. Always have," I admitted in her ear as I got into a rhythm.

"Always have. Always will," she bragged, her enticing titties bouncing as she mounted me and dug her nails into my back. She fucked me in that bathroom like she hadn't had it in forever. It wasn't love between us, but it was something; an emotion both easy and hard to quantify or describe. Lots of nothing and a little of "something".

But could that "something" be enough?

5-Truth

Paris-Café Charbon in the
11th Arrondissement/Oberkampf area

Most jobs these days had removed the personal element and could be done with little leg work, consisting of a few electronic clicks or screen taps here and there. There is no guidebook for what I do. Many decisions are off gut feeling, but some still require that face-to-face contact to be sure you were right. This was one of those situations. Just like anything bought overseas, it didn't hurt to see the product upfront.

Sophia's selection arrived via Vespa, parking on the corner next to the café. She was late, but that was expected. Since finding her via social media, it took several days of coercion to get her to agree to this meeting, but we had to be patient. Rather, Sophia had to be patient; and I can't tell you how hard that was for my friend. But all my digging and knowledge of the right "fit" for things told me this was the one.

What his name once was didn't matter. His name was Esmé now. I'm man enough to admit it; Esmé was fuckin' beautiful and a stunner in any damn country. From my initial observation, I couldn't tell that she was ever categorized as male. She was certainly what Sophia was looking for. But did Sophia have what Esmé needed?

As Esmé entered the café, she removed her vintage black helmet and shook free her full curly mane. More than a few men took notice of the Algerian light almond complexion, long eyelashes and deep brown eyes set at around five foot seven. With Marvin Gaye's harmonies playing in the background, it was the perfect entrance.

"Damn, bitch look better than me. Werrrrrk it, girl," Sophia smugly muttered, seated beside me in a booth facing the front door. She wore large eyeglasses framed by a wig not her hair color while I was dressed in an expensive navy blue suit and dark sunglasses with temporary tattoos riddling my neck and both hands; certain things people would notice and remember, but which would no longer be associated with us by the evening. We motioned Esmé toward the single chair across the cherry wood table from us. It allowed her ease of escape if she felt this wasn't for her. If this arrangement was to go forward, pressure wasn't going to be the driving force.

Sophia stood up first; exchanging double kisses on the cheek with Esmé as if they were long lost friends. I remained seated and simply nodded, knowing my role.

Sophia spoke in French, "Je vous remercie pour la reunion avec nous."

"Please," Esmé said in pretty fair English as she raised a hand. "Your French accent offends my ears. Did you rehearse that on your way here?"

I stifled a laugh while Sophia breathed a deep sigh behind pursed lips, uncomfortably fidgeting with her false hair.

"What are you? Americans?" Esmé inquired.

"No. Canadian," we blurted out in unison like some old married couple. At least it matched our passports this trip.

"Let's cut to the ludicrous nature of your request. You want me to seduce this American rapper El Jefe Blaque somewhere in the world. Why would I do such an absurd thing?"

"It's not quite that crude or absurd, but your being here tells me you're considering our offer," Sophia bluntly stated, moving it along.

"I've always been naturally curious. It's a fault of mine. But I still have my original question. Why?"

"Because it's best for your future," Sophia replied. "We're offering a lot of Euros for your time and inconvenience. All you have to do is make yourself 'known' then let nature take its course...at least until the time is right."

"Why not somebody that wants this kind of attention?" Esmé resisted as I took note from behind my sunglasses of the cars and passersby out front. There were threats no matter where you went.

"That's just it. Because that would be too obvious. We're not looking for some fame whore with no ethics. This has to be genuine," Sophia stressed, looking all scholarly with her fake prescription eyeglasses.

"Genuine, but you want me to withhold my truth. I've been beaten by men before," she said, her voice wavering and skipping. "Both before and after I was fully 'Esmé'. I won't let it happen again. Not anymore."

"And that's why we're trying to take a stand," I interrupted, feeling the temperature change. "Have you ever listened to his lyrics? El Jefe Blaque is proven to be both sexist and homophobic. Transphobic isn't a reach."

"What are you saying?" Esmé questioned, her attention shifted to me.

"You can take a stand, but would have the funds and means to be free of retaliation from men such as him. You could even donate the money to organizations offering the help and support that you didn't have growing up when coming to terms with your identity; help and support...I didn't have growing up. I grew up in a world less receptive to someone out of tune with who they really are," I preached as I removed my jacket and rolled up one of my sleeves. It revealed the stylized tattoo of a woman's silhouette hidden amongst the others. Honestly, it was just something random the tattoo artist had put on my arm to fill space this morning, but who was I to let it go to waste? "This...this is how I see myself even if it's hidden in plain sight," I continued.

Sophia's mouth dropped just as I kicked her leg under the table.

"You? You're like...," Esmé fumbled, her mouth hanging too.

"Like you? No. I was a coward. I didn't have the guts. Didn't have the support or a world with time for someone who was...is...different," I replied, making my voice softer...more vulnerable.

"So this just isn't about revenge or setting someone up," she decided for herself.

"No. It's about allowing someone to take a stand; even if it seems like a petty job on the surface. When you come forward after showing El Jefe your true self, you will have a platform. Not just for yourself, but for anyone that has feared revealing themselves to the world. Blaque has wealth, fame and adoring groups of fans. If he gets his feelings hurt, he'll move on. But maybe others like him will think twice about how they treat people."

Esmé sat stone-faced in a French sort of way, processing my pitch. A small tear lingered at the outermost corner of her left eye, but it refused to fall. After an eternity, she commented. "I will consider this. Do you have a number where I can call you?"

I gave the slightest of nods to Sophia to resume control. She, in turn, slid a purple colored business card with a local number across the table.

"What is your name?" Esmé asked of me as she stood up to leave.

"Linda. I voudrais que vous m'appeler 'Linda'," I replied.

Esmé tenderly smiled and nodded, her torn jeans quickly turning to leave. "I'll be in touch," she said.

After a nice meal and few celebratory drinks, Sophia and I left Café Charbon.

"If she was a real woman, I wouldn't mind a roll with that," she remarked about Esmé.

"If she was a real woman, I wouldn't mind watching the two of you," I slyly admitted, thinking back to the first time I watched Sophia with a girl. It was many years ago in Vegas on a simple blackmail job where she was playing me.

"You're a mother fucker, man. That was damn impressive what you did back there," my cohort, former model and sometimes lover complimented as we took slow, lazy steps. The romantic aura of Paris was casting its spell even over those who were up to no good.

"The deal was lost. I saved it. Simple enough," I stated with a shrug.

"Still, you almost had me believing you wanted to be a woman."

"That's what I do. Make people believe," I admitted in a rare honest moment. At least Sophia was aware of my true nature and had no reservations about it. A rare quality.

"Well, I gotta apologize for all the grief I've been giving you. You've still got it, Truth. Watching you in action back there made me wet. And I got another confession to make," she uttered softly in my ear.
"Oh?"

"I'm still horny as fuck. That is, if your feminine side don't mind, 'Linda'. You couldn't come up with a sexier sounding alter-ego?" Sophia straight clowned.

"Tres funny. With your *poor French accent*," I teased.

"Let's say we celebrate back at the hotel room and play dress-up. You can keep those tats for a while longer and I can stay in this wig. Room service and all the pussy you can handle, just not in that order."

ERIC PETE

As I accepted her generous offer, something
made the hairs on the back of my neck stand up.
Actually, it was three "somethings". Matching black
Mercedes sedans crammed the already cramped Rue
Oberkampf, two sitting parked behind us on the one
way street, making it difficult for traffic to pass; and
another ahead of us near the corner with Rue Saint-
Maur. I recognized the license plate of one that had
twice driven past Café Charbon while we were inside.
They weren't following Esmé. And Theo Clark's men
didn't know where on Earth we were, so...

"Listen to me," I called out to Sophia as I
pretended to laugh, pulling her close for a kiss. "When
we get to the corner, we're going to cross toward that
photo shop. We need to change out of these clothes
and leave town now."

Before Sophia could protest, the sedan in front
of us surged forward, closing the gap just as the two
Benzes behind us spat out their passengers. Five
imposing, stone-faced men in leather jackets-probably
Russian or Ukrainian-looked to be heavily armed by
their stance and wasted no illusion on what they came
to do.

I quickly crunched the odds and outcomes in my
head, coming to the same conclusion each time.

We weren't going to make it to the corner.

And we probably weren't getting out of here
alive.

6-*Truth*

Sophia clutched my hand as the doors to the Mercedes flung open, two ominous heads rising into view. The men behind us began lowering ski masks over their scowled-up faces, preparing to take aim with the weapons stowed beneath their jackets.

One second.

That's about all the time I had to act. The demographics of the area seemed a little off for what I came up with, but nothing I could do about that.

"Justin Bieber! Justin Bieber!" I shouted at the top of my lungs, confusing Sophia. It startled our hunters even more that I pointed in the direction of the Mercedes in front of us and screamed hysterically, "Oh mon dieu! Dans cette voiture! Je l'ai vu!"

My jumping up and down sold it and in that moment of hesitation, the car in front of us was besieged by a wave of crazed young Parisians trying to get past the *armed bodyguards* to their imaginary passenger. I enjoyed a moment to smirk at the frustrated strangers who were supposed to cut us off, feeling another wave of bodies behind us surging in the same direction.

As me and Sophia were shoved about, I stole another quick glance behind us, expecting those five to retreat, regroup and make another run at us later. Maybe that would give me time to figure out what this was about and, more importantly, who'd sicced these scowling bastards on us.

But the growing hysterical mob wasn't enough to get them off their game. They were trained professionals, but also uncaring mercenaries and three teenagers paid the price, collapsing at our feet. At first, I thought they got tripped up in the rush, but their screams and the streams of crimson flowing onto the sidewalk quickly dashed such hopes. These dudes had no chill and they were shooting kids just to get to us.

"Oh shit! Oh shit!" Sophia mouthed without taking a breath, frantically shuffling her feet to avoid getting blood on her heels. Even in this dire situation, the former model could still go all prissy on me.

Another shot barely missed my head, instead striking a young man square in the middle of his backpack. He tumbled forward, his arms flailing before falling lifelessly into the street with the rest of his body. The poor kid's spine was probably severed. This time, somebody noticed and the mob turned desperate and chaotic with people sprinting for cover amid the screams. My distraction that I thought was oh so smart had turned oh so deadly.

As we crouched low, about to lose any cover we had, I yanked Sophia's wig off her head and swatted the eyeglasses from her face. She almost cursed me out before realizing I'd made her less of a target. "Look. I'll distract them. Follow the crowd away from me and run for the Metro. I'll catch up to you at the hotel. If I'm not there in an hour, you know what to do. Now run!" I ordered. She pivoted to bolt then suddenly halted. Had she been shot?

"What? Go!" I scolded her as the five men behind us began their cautious march, another shot almost striking my leg. These near misses were to keep me in one spot as their Benzes scattered from the scene, bodies bouncing off them as they roared down the street. Their transportation was gone for now, but the men were committed, their ski masks fully pulled down in place.

"I...I love you," Sophia gushed, her pinned hair cascading across her sweaty brow. She seemed as stunned by the words as I. She thought we were going to die.

"I love you too," I replied almost on reflex, visibly shaken while my eyes begged her to get the fuck out of here.

"Boy, that was probably your worst lie ever," she jokingly spouted before placing her soft lips to mine in parting. Sophia ditched her jacket as she gracefully blended into the pandemonium, not doing anything to single herself out in the attackers' sights. *That's my girl*, I proudly thought before darting in the opposite direction, dodging my pursuers' bullets as I fled amidst the stalled bumper-to-bumper traffic along Rue Saint-Maur. Most people had either abandoned their vehicles or were huddled in fear behind locked car doors, praying to be left alone. At least two more innocents were hit and more than a few windshields as I zigged and zagged, running both over and around the tiny cars people loved out here. But I didn't let it deter me. A conscience would've long been the death of me if I truly had one.

And I wasn't ready to die without knowing why someone was willing to shoot up Paris just for me.

I ran as fast as I could toward Avenue de la Republique, knowing their tactics were slow and deliberate. Looking back, they'd begun a steady trot just to keep me in their sights. I ditched my jacket then with another quick burst, I was briefly hidden from them. In that moment, I dove for the ground behind a vegetable truck then rolled underneath. As they sped up to catch me, fearing I'd escaped around the corner, I was instead slithering toward them. Their two fastest men went into a full-on sprint, not noticing me crouching behind the truck's wheel as they blazed past. I came out from under the old truck before the other three caught up and brought my weight down on the door handle of an abandoned cleaning van, breaking the lock. Once inside, I struggled to catch my breath while allowing the tiniest crack with which to spy outside.

Then I listened, hoping the next sound wouldn't be bullets riddling the van's wall and me as well. My lungs burned and my muscles ached, feeling that maybe I'd been in this position far too many times. I'd begun gradually removing myself from this business of blackmail and revenge, but what I'd really become was sloppy.

The clip-clop of Number Three's boots gave him away as he muttered something in Russian. But he was farthest from the sidewalk's edge and, with no gun of mine, out of my reach. Number Two seemed to be on the opposite sidewalk, proceeding a little more cautiously as he looked between cars, a short semi-automatic rifle hanging on his shoulder. I strained to watch through the slit in the door as he called back to who I guess was Number One, probably telling him to do the same. My target did me a favor by yelling back, letting me know he was too close for comfort. He shuffled, lazily dragging his boots before his shadow's arrival on the ground in front of me. Poor guy probably didn't expect this gig to be so troublesome and wasn't in shape for a chase. I took a deep breath, preparing for the stupidity that was about to begin. When I saw the tip of his boot right outside the van, I acted.

With as much force as I could bring, I erupted from the cleaning van swinging out the door and catching the trailing Number One by surprise as I bust him in the face. His hands reached to remove his bloody ski mask just as I brought a heel to his knee, jamming it into an unnatural position. As he howled and cried, I snatched the gun from his holster, a Ruger. Before he gathered his wits to train his automatic weapon on me, I placed the Ruger muzzle under his chin and pulled the trigger. Before lazy Number One hit the ground, I'd already placed two rounds into cautious Number Two across the street. I wanted to take out Number Three before he could radio the rest, but he stayed out of range. When I say range, I meant my range, not his.

Number Three didn't hesitate as he brought his rifle to bear on me and fired. The spray of rounds punctured the van's doors and almost me if I hadn't fallen onto Number One who was now missing a significant piece of his head. I stood back up, firing off a single shot just to keep him at bay, but he was still too far away and I might need the remaining bullets in the clip.

I ran back down Rue Saint-Maur and fled into a parking garage I'd noticed before. On the second floor, I shot open a door to the abandoned offices above. Finding my way up, I figured out how to get to the roof then jumped, going rooftop to rooftop in an effort to avoid any more pursuers before descending a fire escape onto du Chermin Vert.

Inside the Hotel Ibis on Rue de la Folie-Regnault, all the talk was of the senseless shootings mere kilometers away as those familiar French sirens filled the air outside. I used a key to an economy room I rented from month to month, one of many around the world for occasions such as this. That clock in my head was ticking, so I didn't delay as I briskly showered and shaved my head. The dark ink of my temporary tattoos circled the drain along with my hair, removing the final traces of a man who'd recently dined at Café Charbon before being hunted by armed madmen. From the room safe, I retrieved a change of clothes, new phone and a back-up fake ID; setting them all on the bed as I clicked on the TV. Police had the city on alert, telling people to stay indoors while they worked to figure out what happened. Due to the world we lived in, theories of this being terror related were springing up already.

Something about those Russians, Ukrainians or whatever they were felt familiar. I hastily reflected on my most recent jobs, but nothing seemed to warrant retaliation this extreme. Usually innocents were off limits, but somebody had decided to go *scorched Earth*. Congrats to them for they had my attention.

As I rushed out the hotel lobby in my new guise, the TV talking heads had something new to say. It was a name which drew my attention. I slowed down; shaking my head in a display of sadness as any normal person would show; and stood to the back of the small crowd of hotel guests listening intently.

"Could this heinous attack in Paris be linked to the deposed, exiled Sheikh Al-Bin Sada who was found yesterday in an upscale London hotel with his throat

slit, his alleged mistress and security guard bound in the bathroom with single bullets to their heads?" the British woman posed on the BBC feed the hotel was courteous enough to carry.

How had I missed that news?

Oh wait. I was snoozing on the transatlantic flight here with Sophia.

Sophia...whom I'd rescued from that very same Sheikh before.

A wave of nausea overcame me.

I assumed these men were after me, but could Sophia have been their actual target? She'd been operating in my world long enough to accumulate some enemies of her own. Or maybe she still had something of the Sheikh's that people would kill for.

And I'd separated from her; chased her off, thinking she'd be safer that way.

As I stepped outside, nothing seemed off on the street. I tried to call Sophia, but no one answered. Either she was unable to answer or the phone was being jammed. Neither was good. I'd only taken a few steps before browsing the nearby rooftops. A man was up there with binoculars, looking for something or someone. He wasn't police, instead dressed like his newly deceased buddies Number One and Two. Damn sloppy of me to have not considered eyes-on-high earlier. These dudes had cast a wide net and were as patient as me.

They were smart enough to try to take out the Sheikh and us within twenty-four hours rather than alerting me by doing it too soon. I considered unloading what was left of my clip, but with police swarming, couldn't bring any more attention to myself. Instead, when he finally trained his binoculars on the one man looking squarely at him, I nodded then gave him the finger before slipping away.

Their element of surprise was over and I was armed now. I just had to get to Sophia before they did.

Under heavy scrutiny by the French police, I boarded the Paris Metro line 3, taking it to the Levallois-Perret commune in the northwest suburbs. While I seemed calm on the outside, I had the same fears as the general public, except mine were of a more intimate nature. The Anatole France Station was closer to Hotel Renard, where we were supposed to meet, but whoever these people were might be waiting for me to emerge right there. I decided to exit one stop early and came above ground at Louis Michel Station, walking past well-armed French special ops police posted there to keep the peace.

Sophia was to be waiting in a black Citroën C5 at a predetermined spot with the engine running. Just blocks away, I saw nothing had changed in those plans. And with five minutes to spare, I allowed some relief to creep in. Her back was turned to me, probably listening to Beyoncé way too loud as she checked her nails or something, figuring everything was going to be okay. Maybe I'd spoiled her into thinking there was nothing I couldn't do. In hindsight, I wished she'd have just looked in the rearview mirror to see what kind of fucked up shit was upon her.

You see, I learned Sophia wasn't the only one waiting for me.

One of the Mercedes from earlier came skidding around the corner, as I was two blocks away from our escape. The French police outside the Metro station noticed the car and began chasing it on foot, but it was already rushing toward me. I kept walking as normal as I could, pretending I didn't hear the revving engine until the last minute. Figuring I was about to get run over, I spun around and fired one shot into the windshield.

Of course it was bullet proof.

As it jumped the curb, I instead dashed into the street, figuring I might have a chance if I just said "fuck it" and ran in a straight line. I only had one block to go after all. When it got close enough for me to be certain I wouldn't miss, I jumped aside and emptied my clip on the car's front tire, blowing it out.

Behind the tinted windows, the driver lost control and overshot me, swerving into the intersection where it was t-boned by a delivery truck. The police were hustling to catch up, yelling at me to stop and put my hands up. Instead, I sprinted into the intersection and ran around the car wreck, toward Sophia outside the hotel. I was almost to her, ready to pull off another great escape when a Mercedes SUV headed off Sophia's car.

I was out of bullets and no match for whatever they were probably packing, but at least I had the Citroën to stage at least a car chase to freedom. I liked my odds with that and it gave me an extra rush of adrenaline.

"Sophia!" I yelled, not bothering if anyone heard her real name at this point. Now if only she'd turned down the music or at least noticed the SUV.

A single man exited the Benz buggy, but was too far to stop me from reaching my destination. He was unusually tall and unlike the others, he dared to smile. Taking my final steps, I reached my hand out for the car door handle. This man motioned with his hand, waiting for this very moment to snatch victory from my fingers. Someone inside the SUV's backseat responded, lowering their window. I remember seeing a tube protruding out the window and aimed in our direction.

"God, no. They wouldn't," I raggedly mouthed in astonishment as a plume of smoke and brief blast of flame erupted from it.

Then my world erupted into something worse.

"Sophia—"

ERIC PETE

7-Truth

He drank deeply from his glass of water, getting those golden vocal cords ready. All the conversation in the college arena ceased on demand. Shareholders, employees, tech reporters, geeks and wannabes gleefully sat on the edge of their seats. I think we were pretending to be Pinnacle Products employees, or *P Squares* as they liked to call themselves, but stood out among the tiny handful of black people in here.

"What we're talking about today is a revolutionary way of communicating with one another. A paradigm shift in how we do things," the self-absorbed man in the mock turtleneck droned as he tracked back and forth across the stage.

Sophia sat like she was hinging on his every word while I toyed with my fake ID badge from behind my Malcolm X glasses. This was Sophia's first solo job and she was eager for it to get to the good part.

"Ladies and gentlemen, the future is now!" the middle-aged technology guru announced as the lights in the audience dimmed and his PowerPoint presentation began.

But the unveiling of Pinnacle's newest gadget wasn't going to be quite as revolutionary as he'd touted. Matter of fact, what the audience was about to be introduced to was something far more basic.

"How much?" the man in the grainy video asked while we watched. The man on stage was just as confused by everyone else, motioning to his tech squad to fix it ASAP.

"First off, no kissing. Twenty five for hand job. Fifty for blow job. One for the real deal...condoms only. One fifty for anal. Two for anything and everything you like, baby," the prostitute replied as he stared directly at her breasts. Idiot didn't know he was also looking into a camera. If you will, *smile for the booby* rather than *smile for the birdie*. It took four camera equipped prostitutes and a week of waiting before getting footage Sophia could use.

"You think you're worth that much?" the man on screen haggled, his voice surprisingly similar to the presenter's.

"Oh. I know I am," she bragged. *"This pussy will get you in trouble if you ain't careful."* Truer words were never said.

"You're a dirty little black slut, aren't ya?" our friend touted in a phrase that would be relayed by

everyone in attendance and echoed across the internet.

"I can be anything you like, sweetie. Just as long as your money's long."

"Shut it off! Shut it off!" he yelled as he ran around in circles, imploring them to turn on the lights in here and get rid of his former adoring fans. The more he panicked, the more erratic he became. It was almost like he was having a psychotic breakdown. The little something extra in his glass of water ensured that, making for a few more memorable moments he'd never live down.

"Congratulations," I said, shaking Sophia's hand. She was creative with her compensation terms for this job, accepting stock options in Pinnacle that would be tanking by morning. But it, as well as her stock, would bounce back under new leadership; or maybe just the return of the right leadership at the helm. Like perhaps the black woman who he'd unfairly robbed of her position on the board through lies and deceit; a visionary who wasn't going to take this shit without a fight and maybe some creative ideas for revenge.

Yeah, people like Sophia and I served a purpose.

"This is how it feels?" Sophia asked, continuing to hold my hand amid the laughter and mumbling of everyone in attendance.

"Sometimes," I replied. "Other times, I just put the job behind me and don't look back. They usually aren't feel good stories or happy endings."

"Thank you," she said.

"Huh? For what?" I questioned. She'd done this one all on her own.

"For giving me purpose," she remarked, this strange, serene smile dotting her face. As beautiful as she was, Sophia always sought approval. And perhaps, someone to look out for her. Despite her originally coming into my life on a lie, part of someone's failed revenge on me, I'd found us to be alike; both talented yet flawed.

Maybe I was the way I am because nobody truly looked out for me. Maybe by keeping her close, she might become something more. Perhaps something better.

Because while I surely did some things well, I had failed as a human being.

"What's wrong?"

"Nothing," I answered, clutching her hand a little more tightly. "Not a thing."

I turned toward Sophia, daring to smile back. But something was different and not how I remembered things. Smoke began rising up from her hair followed by rivers of blood flowing from her scalp. Then, as flames arose, her face began to melt right before my eyes. While this happened, she didn't say a word. No sound. Not even a scream.

And then she was gone, consumed in a blinding flash and deafening boom.

My ears rang like someone was blowing a loud whistle inside my skull and I could barely see two inches in front of me.

"Monsieur!" I could finally comprehend, blinking as the frightened man shook me from a bad dream. It was so, so hard to think. Words ran together in my head like pools of mush of which I couldn't make any sense.

"*What? Why are they speaking French? Am I in Mali again? No. Too many white faces. And why am I in a hotel?*" I thought as I went to push off to rise to my feet. But my right arm wouldn't cooperate. Then I realized that was because it was pinned beneath the burning remnants of a car door.

Wait...

"Sophia!" I screamed, finishing my thought from who knows how long before I somehow wound up in this hotel lobby. But how did I get here? And where was Sophia?

A brave woman from the hotel staff joined the man, using their jackets to safely drag the car door off my arm. I still couldn't move it though and almost ignored the fire draping my sleeve if it hadn't become so painful. I frantically swatted at it with my other hand just as the sprinklers came on, the cool drops serving to further jar my memory from its dulling fog.

I labored to move and strained my neck just to turn toward the street out front. Rue Aristide Briand was easy to see through the large hole blown in the hotel's facade, allowing the smoke and flames to blow inside.

Gazing at my mangled arm, I remembered reaching for the door handle. Then the tall man in the black SUV smiled. Someone used a rocket launcher of some sort. Then... Sophia.

I guess I did get my hand on the Citroën's handle after all. But the explosion blew the door off, taking me with it as we hurtled through the large windows of the hotel lobby.

"Do you know what happened?" another man asked as he nervously watched the gaping hole, probably fearful of more masked gunman roaming the streets of Paris.

"No. I was walking by," I grunted in French as I tried to stand once more. My burned arm was probably fractured and the rest of me didn't feel much better. A bottle of pain pills and a glass of whiskey were needed right away.

The sirens got louder as a city stretched thin by this shit was finding a way to stretch just a little more.

There would be lots of questions and I wasn't even on my C game, let alone an A game.

But first I had to see.

"Is anyone else alive out there?" I asked as I tried to hobble along, keeping some hope.

"You really shouldn't go out there. Paris is a mess and it's not safe. And you're hurt," the older man chided in more of a Swiss-French accent.

"Yes. A car in front blew up, causing all this. There's another car at the corner that was in a terrible wreck. Between all of this and what they did at Oberkampf, these terrorists are despicable!" a woman spat for her reply as she wiped soot from her face.

I placed a handkerchief across my nose & mouth and waded into the thick black smoke blowing in my face. My unsteady steps were labored with dread on top of physical pain, but I pressed on. Outside, the Mercedes SUV was gone, but its handiwork remained. The sky seemed to take on a shade of red, making the Citroën wreckage even more eerie, the flames too intense to get any closer. A charred body was a taunting lesson that there was no way Sophia escaped. It hurt too much to cry otherwise I would've.

"Monsieur, you're getting too close," someone from the hotel softly reminded me as I felt prickly pain on my cheek. My arm had gone numb now and I stumbled back, exhaustion winning over will. "Please. You need medical attention. Come back inside."

"Yes, you're right," I said as I backed up under what was left of the awning, leery of any rooftop cameras that might be watching. There was already enough surveillance video of me on the street outside Hotel Renard to raise questions. The fake ID I had in my pocket would stand to basic scrutiny, but under these heightened conditions?

Two fire engines arrived, accompanied by an ambulance with three police cars and a bomb squad van leading the way. I had to admire that these people didn't know what to expect, but were still charging in to render aid.

Knowing it was best that I get the fuck outta here, I quit talking and let the EMTs render aid while the Police Nationale questioned the more able-bodied people about what they saw.

"Monsieur, do you know who was in that car outside?" one of them asked, leaning my way. Outside, the fire engine was dousing the car. His detective eye noticed by my scorched appearance that, out of everyone in here, I must've been closest to the explosion.

"No," I softly answered with a lie in French, shaking my head as well. "I was just standing. Don't...don't know what happened."

"Are you a guest at this hotel?" he followed, his attention now ratcheted up. He was committing my features and clothing to memory for whenever he got around to surveillance video later.

"No...I," I began before wincing in pain at the medic's touch. Oh, the pain in my arm was real, but I just chose to emphasize it.

"We need to get him to the hospital," the medic alerted the police, having seen enough of my condition. He motioned for his partner to wheel the stretcher over.

"I'll get the information from you later," the officer relented with a wave of his head, stepping aside for the stretcher.

Not if I can help it, I fiendishly thought as I was rolled outside.

Some French media had already arrived, giving the Police Nationale more than a handful as they hastily cordoned off the area. In the back of the ambulance, I was given oxygen while my attendant went about further assessing my burned arm.

"Monsieur, I'm going to give you a sedative because this may hurt," he said as he reached back into a supply drawer.

"No. No sedative," I pleaded with a wave of my left arm, already succumbing to the concussion I knew I had. What if those same mother fuckers realized I wasn't dead and were watching? If unconscious, I'd be powerless to stop them. Not that I was much of a threat in this condition, but...

"It'll be okay," he said, trying to calm me. "I'm going to secure you for the ride to the hospital first, so nothing happens during transport."

As I fought to keep my arm free, there was a loud slap on the outside of the ambulance that startled both of us. I half-expected my pursuers to fling the door open and let their guns blaze, but there were too many police and reporters around here to be that brazen. I think. I'd already been proven wrong once today.

"Do you have room for another?" one of the police asked, peering in the door.

"We're spread thin. I guess we have no choice," the attendant replied as he stole a look at his driver.

"Good. We have a survivor from the car wreck at the corner. Somehow, someone in that Mercedes lived," the officer commented, his eyes enlarging as he exaggerated his surprise.

Of course, my eyes were suddenly as big, my rage bubbling up.

8-Truth

"Careful. He's dangerous," the officer stated as they loaded another stretcher beside me. "I'm radioing ahead for extra people at the hospital."

"You think he's one of those terrorists?" the attendant gasped, not expecting the apparent white features before him. The newest passenger was barely moving with a horribly swollen face and faint breathing, a deep moan emanating from below his oxygen mask. Seeing as they tried to run me over, and failed, I took some joy in that.

"Don't know for sure, but we recovered weapons from what's left of their car," the officer admitted. "And ski masks. Be sure to keep him alive as long as possible. Maybe we can get some answers."

They were so concerned about securing the bloodied man that they'd forgotten about tying me down. I slid the straps over my arm, pretending I was firmly in place. They even forgot my sedative.

Once underway, my attendant spent more time curiously watching the other one. I was watching him too though, wondering who he was and who hired him. But I needed some meds to keep me going.

"Everything okay back there?" the driver asked.

"Oui. Number two's vitals are weak, pulse is erratic. Internal injuries are significant from what I can tell," the attendant admitted.

"What about number one? Is he sedated?"

"Mon Dieu! I almost forgot! Merci."

It was time and I'd heard enough. I grimaced, making sure he saw my discomfort. As expected, he reached over the other man, retrieving a needle packet.

"Bet you're ready for this now," he commented while I steadily groaned. I kept my free arm tucked in, waiting patiently for him to come closer.

He reached to roll up my sleeve and that's when he realized my strap wasn't secured. Just as he hesitated, I chopped him in his windpipe then snatched the needle from his hand. With a quick flip of direction, I jabbed it as fast as I could into him and injected the sedative. It was hard doing all this with one good arm, but the man was a civilian and I was motivated. As he fell away from me, I grasped at his jacket just in time.

I strained my neck to see if the driver noticed any of this, but he was busy radioing the hospital. I slowly pulled the attendant forward until he fell against me. His eyes were glazed, but he was fighting it. Probably another shot needed to really put him out. Improvising, I banged his head on the stretcher rail to get the job done.

I discretely cleared my throat then carefully considered my next words. "Remy!" I called out, doing my best worst impression of the attendant.

"What?" Remy the driver replied.

"Pull over. I need help with the second patient," I instructed in French, using the attendant's body to shield my face. To the driver, I gambled it simply looked like his coworker's back was turned to him.

"Are you sure? We're almost to the hospital and he's probably going to die anyway. Fucking terrorist bastard; He's probably from the Balkans," he cursed.

"You heard what the inspector said. They need him alive longer. Get back here now," I coaxed, hoping the engine noise masked my voice enough.

Just like his friend, the driver fell for the okie-doke. This time I played on the driver's paranoia, screaming wildly as I claimed the other man was conscious and faking it. Fearful of the hunter in black rather than man who was black, the driver's back was turned and it took just a little more effort to incapacitate him. But in the struggle, I think I further injured myself. After shooting myself up with a pain killer and wrapping my maimed arm in gauze bandages, I stripped the EMTs of their clothes, leaving them sedated and tied together with the stretcher restraints.

With the ambulance lights flashing and my hat pulled low, I drove right past Centre Médical Inter Europe Paris and kept going. My mode of transportation along with a bit of quick thinking got me past a few checkpoints, but the ambulance radio kept squawking. Being overdue at the hospital gave me only a limited amount of time, so I knew not to remain in it much longer. Turning off my lights and siren, I parked inside a tiny garage on a quiet street in the 19th Arrondissement.

My hunter might die, but not before I had a moment or so with him to myself.

He couldn't talk, even after I shot him up with Epinephrine. And he had no ID. But his body's dark, rich tattoos had a voice of their own. The Madonna with the baby Jesus was sprawled in great detail across his chest, but this dude was about as religious as me. Removing his pants, I found two eight sided stars, one on each knee. They symbolized he'd rather die than kneel before the authorities. No wonder they weren't fearful of a body count. If he wasn't Russian, he was from around those parts or at least spent time in their prisons. Probably a Vor v Zakone or "Thief in Law" as those kinds were known.

Having all I could get from him, I removed his oxygen mask and yanked his cervical collar off, hurling it across the ambulance in a fit of frustration. Nature would take its course. I paused for a moment to watch him convulse, but his final moments weren't important. I'd save that view for whoever was behind this. Only then would I properly mourn Sophia.

I exited the garage on foot, wearing mismatched clothes and carrying enough medicine to get me by. But I couldn't fake a healthy arm and too many people had seen me up close. Some more funds and another change of ID would be nice, but more importantly, I needed some way out this country to convalesce and get a handle on things.

And my salvation came courtesy of a poster taped to a street light. Inspecting it closer, it was for the Jonas Barfield tour. Last night was the pop singer's final show in Paris before the next leg of his tour. I recalled Sophia begging me to go last night. "Focus on your job," I'd chided her, promising we'd catch the show in Toronto or something.

But that wasn't possible anymore.

Adjusting my hat, I clenched my jaw then hobbled along.

ERIC PETE

9-Truth

"Did you see my message to the people of Paris? It was dope, huh?" he asked in a syrupy drawl, having already arrived at his own answer. He glided in ahead of her, his wiry frame possessing a smooth grace even away from the stage, always the consummate showman.

"Oui," was her simple reply. Her French indifference struck just the right chord in the face of his gargantuan ego.

I mean, no shade, Jonas Barfield had carved out his niche in the entertainment world. Originally a member of the boyband Saint Roch; the edgy, urban white boy with the angelic smile had blossomed into a solo megastar with worldwide crossover appeal. This young millionaire had a lot to show for his multitude of talents-a bunch of awards, platinum albums, minor acting roles and a hot ass Victoria's Secret model for a fiancé. Yeah, the sole white dude from the boyband was on another level while the three brothers were left with "We still here" tours and late night infomercials.

"I stand with all y'all, but especially with you," he said wrapping her up in a hug. "Damn you sexy, girl," he lustfully praised in her ear as one of his boys entered with a clipboard and pen. "My fiancé can't find out about this though. You okay with the non-disclosure agreement before we get down to business?" he asked as he gently nudged her toward the outstretched pen.

His expected conquest hesitated, forcing down her revulsion before snatching the pen from Jonas' handler and quickly scribbling her name and signature on the piece of paper.

"Alright! That's what I'm talking about. This is gonna be a special night in the City of Light," he cheered with the formalities out the way, motioning for his people to bounce and wait for him downstairs.

I knew Jonas Barfield from his On-Phire Records days. You see, Jason North, the former head of the record label, was responsible for putting the band Saint Roch together. Jason had vision for he was also the first person to put my talents to use. Or maybe misuse, since he was family of mine. Close family even, but that's perhaps another story for another time. Yeah, I got issues.

Jonas was always the cautious one in terms of his image, so it took a lot in this climate to coax him out his plush five star accommodations to something riskier where I waited.

But throughout history, pussy has been a hell of a motivator. Wars have been fought and lost over that shit.

You might say it trumps all reason in men.

Or at least the promise of it...because poor Jonas wasn't getting any tonight under any circumstance.

I quietly waited as the curly haired kid with manscaped eyebrows got comfortable on her dark blue velour sofa, clicking through the French TV channels for a rebroadcast of his message to the people of Paris. If they were any good, his handlers were probably embedding the YouTube clip on his fan page.

His lady friend's sullen eyes beside him met mine from the sofa and, not dallying any longer, she placed a gentle kiss on his lips before getting up and walking away. Jonas was left confused, his outstretched arms lingering with nothing to grasp. "Oh, you want me to follow you! Well alright then!" he eagerly cheered, clapping his hands together before kicking his shoes off.

As I emerged from my vantage point in the hallway, Esmé slapped the fuck out of me, reminding me, behind the soft and sultry exterior, there was still a bit of man in there. In my current state, getting my bell rung wasn't so good and I think I wobbled a bit.

"You are a despicable bastard whoever you are. When I come out, I want you all to be gone. For good," she spat in French before entering her bedroom and slamming the door behind her. I deserved it for what I had her say and do tonight to get Jonas here. But I probably deserved it more for betraying her trust. That set of lies from Café Charbon had easily rinsed away with my tattoos, but she remained stained by my hollow words and how I'd inspired her. I was still gonna pay her like Sophia had planned for the original job. But necessity called for a change being a job I needed instead that she now was unable to refuse. Esmé knew those attacks began in Oberkampf right after she left us, but was too fearful to bring it up directly with me. I didn't particularly like it, but used it to my advantage when I showed up at her doorstep.

"Truth?" Jonas gasped, almost tumbling off the sofa like he'd seen a ghost. I half expected to see a yellow stain pooling in his white pants.

"Long time no see, white boy," I teased with a wicked smile, trying to project menace through a medicated fog.

"She your girl? Look man. I didn't know," he stuttered as he scrambled to right himself on the couch, trying to exchange the falsetto in his throat for some timely bass.

"Nah. This is about business. And logistics. You still got that big ass entourage and road crew you travel with?" I questioned.

"Yeah. I gotta go to London in the morning, yo. Next stop on the tour. Why? You need front row seats?" he asked, trying to feign generosity.

"Cancel it. Shit's crazy out there. Of course you know that already, Mr. Barfield," I uttered, mocking his solidarity PR stunt that was airing again on the TV news.

"Cancel? That'd be messing with my money. Is you crazy?" he dared, almost uttering the N- word as he tried to stand up. When I took another step closer, he sat right back down.

"I think you need to head home. To be with your fiancé in times like this. I can see you're distraught and missing her. I mean, why else would you be here seeking comfort in another woman's arms? Or rather between her legs," I poked, slightly grimacing as I went to fold my arms out of habit.

"What's wrong with your arm, man?" he asked, finally realizing I wasn't one hundred percent.

"A minor disagreement. You should see the other guy. On second thought, you probably shouldn't," I replied, trying to regain my scariness with his eyes.

"Bro, you don't look so hot. What you need, Truth? Some money?" he asked. "Because I can get something wired to your bank account."

"Bitch, don't play. This ain't about money. I already told you what I need. I need you to cancel your tour. Do you really think just because Jason North is dead that everything he had on you boys is gone too?" I posed, getting in his face so he could see how serious I was. I added a backhand slap, with my good arm, for the exclamation point. "You need to think real careful, kid. Because I ain't the one to piss off."

"Look...man. That wasn't me with them under-aged girls back then. I was never down with that shit," Jonas relented, wilting before the pressure.

"And we can stick with that story, Jonas. You can go on living your life and never set foot on stage...or in a courtroom with your bandmates ever again," I said as I patted him on the shoulder. "Call your boys downstairs and tell 'em you're done with your romantic date."

"That quick?" he rejected, actually offended. Like I said, boy was hung up on perception.

"Trust me. The surprise tonight wasn't in your pants, but hers," I rudely remarked.

∞

The next day, at a private airfield near LAX, Jonas Barfield returned home to much fanfare, his fiancé greeting him with tears in her eyes as the paparazzi ate it up. And off another less-heralded plane in the next hangar, I stepped onto US soil as a member of his road crew. "Round two," I muttered to myself as I separated from the group.

To know just how far the enemy is willing to go is to know them.

It was time to let them get to know me.

ERIC PETE

10-Last Year

Prague, Czech Republic

After several days of helicopter flights and long dusty rides in the dark, he'd finally been put on a plane to an unknown destination. The days of questioning by faceless men then being shuttled to dank, sweaty rooms where forced to sit in silence had disoriented him. Where the torture in that dungeon didn't break him, he now considered suicide if given the chance. He was not going to allow himself to be chained up again like an animal by Third World barbarians.

Along the drive, he tried to remember sounds and sensations, hoping he could tell where he was at. The smooth ride indicated to him somewhere with modern roads, but the smells coming in from the cracked windows threw him off, a mix of new and old world. Rather than the ubiquitous call to prayer he'd endured, his ears were besieged with the pumping and thumping of electronic dance music. In that rare moment, he grinned, not knowing which unnerved him more. As the car slowed, the ride changed to that of an uneven surface; maybe cobblestone streets in an older part of town.

After another few minutes, the ride stopped. He felt his gut lurch as he prepared for another change in environment, fearing it might be the end of the line. They yanked the hood off his head, giving him mere seconds for his eyes to adjust, before swiftly dragging him out the car and through an alleyway door. Struggling to get his feet under him, the three large men dumped him onto the concrete floor. He groaned as he cautiously stood, expecting someone to strike him down. But they kept their hands off him.

He was in a kitchen, maybe at the back of a bar or restaurant, but the staff was absent. A tall man sat on a stool slicing an apple with a pocket knife. While impeccably dressed head-to-toe in black with expensive shoes, they were only window dressing on a stiff-jawed gorilla. While indifferently chomping on a slice, others hastily mopped up a pool of blood on the floor behind him and dragged a body away as if nothing was wrong. He told himself this was for show, something to make him more compliant, but his gut told him it was an all too real day in the life for them.

"My men tell me you claim to be Nathan Piatkowski. Is that your true name?" the tall blonde polar bear of a man asked.

"Yes," he answered.

"Piatkowski," he repeated as if retrieving a memory. "Jew?"

"Yes," Piatkowski replied, tensing up again. He hadn't engaged in much physical activity since his glory days in the field yet prepared for whatever was to come. Even anti-Semitism.

"You're lucky Al-Bin Sada didn't kill you," he dryly noted, exchanging a smile with his men. "Do you know who I am?"

"The person who's letting me live a while longer?" Piatkowski quickly answered, daring to stretch his arms a little.

"Good answer. So...tell me why I should continue to let you live," the man posed, a hint of Russian lacing his English. Perhaps these men were the Russian mob.

"Because you spent time and resources to bathe me, make me look presentable and fly me out of the Middle East. Neither you nor your men strike me as the Good Samaritan types," he dared to joke.

"And you would be correct. So what are you? A mercenary? CIA?" his host guessed.

"Honestly, I don't know what I am now. My family is gone. My wife and son died in a car wreck while I was *indisposed*, thinking I was either dead or had abandoned them. The Sheikh's men were sure to present that news to me between my weekly beatings," he replied, anger for a certain man refueling his tank for vengeance.

"My deepest sympathies, but we're here to do business...or maybe not. The people who found you assumed you were an asset. And I paid good money for their find. So I need to know if you are of some value to me," the man stated as he fully stood, presenting an even more imposing figure. Whereas Piatkowski was around six foot one, he had to be five to six inches taller.

"I'll cooperate fully and give you all I know about the Sheikh, his holdings and interests. As well as offer my expertise in other areas around the world," Piatkowski proclaimed looking up at him.

"And? In return for your 'devotion', I assume you want revenge on Al-Bin Sada."

"Yes," he readily confirmed. "But I also want your help in finding the black bastard who turned me over to the Sheikh in the first place."

"Really? What is he? A government operative? A former coworker you pissed off?"

"No. Some form of freelancer," he reluctantly admitted, seeing his tormentor's face that final time in a Cleveland hotel room. *Good-bye, Mr. Smith*, the nigger had smugly uttered as the Sheikh's men held him down. That was the last time he saw America. "People hire him for his skills. But I tried to force him into a job I needed done...and wound up where you found me."

"He showed you, eh? Tell me...this black man. What is his tradecraft?"

"Revenge, blackmail, deception, escape," he surmised. "He's not a killer as far as I can tell. But he might as well be from his results. I thought I was pretty devious, but he's the fucking devil. I need him dead."

"This black for hire, is he an American?" the man asked, stabbing his knife into the remainder of his apple.

"Yes... I mean. I think he is. He's sort of like a ghost. I couldn't even find a birth certificate or medical records to go along with his fingerprints," he admitted, feeling an unnerving tremble through his body. He'd looked death in the eye many a time over his CIA career. How he could he be rattled by someone who wasn't even a killer?

The tall man left the kitchen island and approached him. His men tensed up like something was wrong, but he calmed them with a wave of his hand. Piatkowski clenched his fists, but knew he was too weak and ineffective for whatever was to come at this man's hands. Had he sunk so low in life?

Rather than landing at his throat, the large hands grasped his shoulders and shook him; not with malice, but enthusiasm. "You can call me 'Dimitri'," the large bear in expensive clothes huffed, peering into his eyes. "You will give me all you know and I will lend my network throughout Europe to deal with Al-Bin Sada permanently, but first I need to know more about this Black Ghost. I think we suddenly have mutual interests, Nathan Piatkowski."

"Piatkowski is dead; and for the better. Please. Call me 'Mr. Smith'," he requested.

"Very well, *Mr. Smith*," Dimitri laughed, his men following suit. "After your trip, you must be starving. Let me fix you some dinner. But first we drink. I hope your weak stomach can handle real Russian Vodka."

11-Last Week

London, England

It took a month for the Sheikh's security detail to get comfortable with the new room service staff. That meant a month of routine frisks, metal detectors, food tasting, and frayed nerves. But the staff was made up of professionals; well paid for their discretion by the Five-Diamond hotel where Sheikh Al-Bin Sada chose to reside in exile, so they endured.

And because Dimitri paid them even better and demanded even more, when guard was let down, it was not going to be them.

Where the Sheikh once commanded an elaborate retinue of no less than fifty and an impressive harem of the most exotic and beautiful women to match, his circle was greatly diminished yet steadfast in their devotion. While the entire fourteenth floor of the hotel on the Strand was rented out, they usually gathered in only two to three of the suites, switching every few days.

The smallest, most "British" of Dimitri's men were chosen for their less intimidating appearance, easily doubling as the utmost gentlemen. This day, the four man team of servants brought a woman along, sending her alone to the Sheikh's suite where he dwelled with his most faithful protector and the lone survivor of his harem. The blonde would be sure to catch the easily bored Al-Bin Sada's eye while they served his seven man detail in the adjacent room.

"Good morning, sirs. Will it be alright to enter?" she asked genially enough with a nervous grin. The large Polynesian who'd spent the greater part of his life in service to the Sheikh grunted, motioning her in. Before allowing her much further inside, he stuck his head into the hallway on reflex. When he was satisfied nothing was amiss, he closed the door, granting her further access. "I have three breakfast orders," she recited, spying the Sheikh in his traditional dishdash and keffiyah folded in the style of his homeland as he stared out at the London skyline, his mind a continent away. Soon, he'd begin diverting a portion of his immense wealth to fund a counter revolution back home, but for now he'd enjoy the English politeness, knowing his days of visiting the US ended years ago.

"I'll check the Prince's plate," the bulky bodyguard instructed to the room service woman as she gawked at the beautiful nude Persian admiring her diamond bracelet without a shred of modesty. Of course the Sheikh still had a wife, but she was being cared for separately in Geneva. The woman at Prince Al-Bin Sada's side was given the name Ahmar, Arabic for red. Once there was another whose beauty could challenge Ahmar within his harem, but the astonishing Aswad was spirited away from under his nose back in Miami by a black American. Those were so much better times. Maybe the black's boss, the Jew he'd held in his dungeon rather than swiftly killing, had cursed him after all. At least the rebels, with their hardliner tendencies, surely had dispatched the infidel. That is if he didn't succumb to starvation.

"Very good, Sir. I have to see which plate is his," the room service attendant with the name tag MARY offered as she knelt down toward the hot box beneath the serving cart table.

"No, I'll do it," the Polynesian instructed as he rudely brushed her aside. Although the outer layer of security in the next suite had probably cleared her, one could never be too certain about bombs or explosives. He had to squat low, but as he reached for the hot box door handle, it flew open behind the force of a foot. He stumbled back onto his butt, scooting clear of a knife blade that followed. As the smallest man on Dimitri's team, uncurled and launched himself toward the Sheikh's bodyguard, he was met with a devastating leg kick from a tree trunk that shouldn't be that fast or that flexible. Room Service Mary pretended to be stunned and backed away toward the door and safety. Ahmar dove across the bed and scrambled toward the room phone as the Prince turned from his thoughts to face the danger head on. He motioned to Ahmar to put the phone down, confidently figuring this would be over soon. Once

Manu broke the little spider-like man, his team of men in the next room would pick apart the carcass. There hadn't been much challenge in London, so this would allow them to stretch their legs at least.

Manu was back to his feet as the attacker thrust his knife toward the large man's ribs. He missed and the bodyguard made him pay for it, swallowing his wrist in his massive grip just before hefting the flexible man over his head and chucking him off the suite wall. Manu smiled as the man dropped his blade, gasping for air. First he was going to crush the man's knife hand for his audacity then rip out his throat and watch him gurgle. True to his plan, Manu stomped on the hand and in the next move had the attacker's tiny neck already relenting to his grip. As he listened for the popping of cervical vertebrae, he'd ignored Room Service Mary who'd fled out the front door. He also ignored the four-man team who took her place, black gas masks still affixed from their mission next door and holding silencer-tipped guns. Just as he squished the last bit of life from the bug, one of them placed a single bullet through the back of Manu's skull, knowing his type would never surrender. Manu died with a smile though and both bodies, big and little, fell to the floor in unison.

Ahmar screamed mightily, suddenly clutching a sheet to her body as if it were protection against a round. A fifth man in a gas mask entered the room with a protesting Room Service Mary in his grasp. He motioned for the others to grab Ahmar at gunpoint, stowing both women in the bathroom for now.

"Don't hurt her," the Prince stated in perfect English as he stabbed a finger toward them. "I assume you want me," he guessed. In response, the fifth man produced a laptop which he set on the table.

"The codes to your European accounts, your Highness," the new man instructed in his muffled voice as the laptop screen lit up. The Prince feared that his men in the next room were no longer with the living, but perhaps he could hire these industrious individuals to replace them. After short consideration, he gave them the requested information to his European accounts. It was only a tiny fraction of his total wealth after all.

As the confirmations came through, the man at the table quickly diverted the money to several discrete funds from a list on his cell phone. *Probably a glorified accountant*, the Prince thought as he watched the swift key strokes with disdain.

"When this is done, I wish to speak with you gentleman as well as your employer about opportunities," Al-Bin Sada teased, his hands parted to show he bore no hostility. While regretting the loss of dear Manu, as long as he and Ahmar walked away, it was a loss he was prepared to endure. At least until he learned these men's identities. Then they would beg for his mercy.

The final transaction was completed in less than four minutes, causing the man at the table to nod to the one nearest the bathroom. That man delivered a simple tap-tap on the bathroom door then stepped away. From inside, a full scream ended abruptly, silenced by a single gunshot. The Sheikh couldn't hide his gasp. From out of the bathroom emerged a smiling Room Service Mary, no longer seeming so frail and nervous. And in her hand was a nine millimeter, a bit of smoke lingering from its barrel.

"No! No! No! Ahmar!" the Sheikh howled, deep sorrow bellowing from his gut over a woman he cared about more than his own wife or even his country. The fifth man stood up from behind the laptop and engaged Al-Bin Sada, yanking his keffiyah from atop his hand and shoving him against the window.

"You thought this was just a robbery, your Highness?" the masked man snarled as he jammed his gun against the heavier man's sweaty temple. Then Mr. Smith yanked his gas mask off, revealing his face to his former tormentor. "You should have killed me when you had the chance, you smug bastard," he hissed before spitting in the Sheikh's face.

The Sheikh wanted to wipe the spittle from his eye but didn't dare flinch; not with a gun to his head and knowing the man he tortured wouldn't hesitate to use it. Mr. Smith whistled a little tune, something he'd do while hanging in that dungeon, then took a blade he'd concealed up his other wrist and dragged it deeply across the Sheikh's throat. As Al-Bin Sada's life slipped away, the pristine white of his dishdash supplanted by a ruby red, Mr. Smith turned to let him tumble onto the hotel room carpet.

While the others unceremoniously stowed one of their own back into the cart's hotbox and proceeded to remove all traces of their presence here, Mr. Smith called Dimitri.

"The transfers went through. Well done," Dimitri complimented upon answering. "Some of this will go towards my expenses tracking that Sophia woman's activities. Chernyy Prizrak...The Black Ghost. Are you certain he'll be in France?" Dimitri anxiously inquired.

"Yes because he's never too far from Sophia. That's how I first caught up with him; when he sprung her from the Sheikh's harem back in America," Smith replied as he peered into the bathroom to make sure Ahmar was dead. There was always the risk that Room Service Mary took pity on her, but no one could be spared. Damn shame for such beauty to die, but she'd hitched her wagon to the wrong horse in the Sheikh. He was going to celebrate this first victory of many in Ahmar's honor by finding and fucking the shit out of someone who resembled her. "She's his weak spot," he added about Sophia, his eyes lingering a bit longer on Al-Bin Sada's favorite.

"You are definitely committed to this cause, Mr. Smith. That is good."

"We're in this together to the end, Dimitri," Smith calmly affirmed, knowing their relationship would end at some point in the future with one of them dead. He wasn't a gullible fool.

"Da. And if we miss him in Europe? What if he somehow slips away this time?" Dimitri proposed.

"I know his weak spots beyond the whore. We go after everyone he holds dear and kill them all. I threatened it before, but this time, I'll do it."

"You remind me of my departed brothers," Dimitri commented with an odd chuckle. "They quarreled to no end, but we were still family. I miss them."

Mr. Smith didn't understand the humor in that. Russians were an odd bunch.

12-Truth

I sat in the local West Seattle chowder house, dividing my attention between the news and Alki Beach across the street.

"Could you turn up the TV?" I asked the bartender as he brought my halibut quesadilla and a Corona.

"Sure thing, my man," he replied as he grabbed the remote and aimed it. "Shoulder surgery?" he inquired as to my arm in the sling.

"Yessir. Pickup game across town at Garfield High. Came down on it wrong. Ain't as young as I used to be," I joked, pretending the searing pain wasn't there. I'd almost dared going straight to my safe house, a condo up the beach where neighbors knew me as a quiet photographer. But I'd done wrong in bringing Sophia there before. Now after what I'd endured in Paris, I couldn't trust that it hadn't been compromised as well. All this time I'd preached to her about not getting lazy when I'd committed that very sin.

And now she was dead.

Letting the finality set in, I wearily rested my head for a moment before focusing on another dose of the 24 hour cable news cycle. On CNN, a few Russian nationals were listed among the victims with the news channel now claiming The Paris Massacre was the result of some "unknown terrorist", perhaps a black male who was a recent convert to the violent ideology.

"Just great. Blame the black guy," I barked a little too loud as my understanding grew of the types of players involved. A gazillion armed masked men wreaking havoc through a European city and somehow it's my fuckin' fault? I mean, I'm pretty impressive when I try, but this? Someone had enough juice to keep the attackers off the news, lump the ones I was lucky to take out in with the victims and somehow pin it on someone who resembled a less handsome me.

The only enemy I'd had with that kind of influence was here stateside, but no longer with us thanks to Al-Bin Sada, may both of them rest in some sort of peace. Still, someone had reach within European government and media to shape this story. Or maybe the authorities were too embarrassed to admit they had no control over their own thugs, so took the easy way out by blaming it on the Brown Terror.

"Crazy, huh?" my bartender commented as talking heads tried to connect dots for their own satisfaction. "Lucky we're here and not over there."

"You got that right. Blessed to say I've never been overseas, I guess," I agreed with a tip of my Corona before taking a deep gulp to wash down the lie.

After finishing my meal, I limped across the street and over to the beach. I took a seat on the bench, gazing upon Puget Sound as a ferry sailed by on its choppy waters.

It wasn't too long before a medium sized olive skinned woman approached with her mutt of a dog. She wore a splash of fuchsia in the middle of her thick dark hair which had grown longer than I remember, but still rebelliously clung to those black Chuck Taylors of hers on her feet. The dog pulled her along until it got close enough to sniff me.

"Hi, Helene," I said, looking up at my neighbor as the dog happily licked my hand.

"What the fuck happened to you, Brandon?" she asked, addressing me by the only name which she'd known me, her face grimacing over my state. At least I'd somewhat cleaned myself up. This sling was the only thing keeping my arm from falling off. "And where's my hug, stranger?"

"You don't know how good that sounds right now, but I can't. Nothing personal," I stated, leading others to believe this was an impromptu conversation between complete strangers. Just in case. "I knew you'd come this way."

"And just how did you know that?"

"On days like this, you always walk Buster down Alki Beach," I admitted, referring to the scruffy dog that was once mine. He had a much better master in the mixed Greek-Duwamish woman with the feisty demeanor.

"Boy, you know his name is Marshawn now. How many times do I have to tell you?" she quickly reminded me.

"Whatever," I remarked with a smile as I continued to rub his head w/ my good hand.

"So where you been this time?" Helene inquired, her pitying eyes not matching the nonchalance in her voice.

"Around. How are things at home?"

"You mean around your crib? And the men who've been asking about you?" she countered. Both her parents were professors at the University of Washington and even if Helene was a non-conformist, you couldn't put anything past her. "You're not a photographer are you?" she stated as less of a question.

"I do take photos...sometimes. And people pay me, so..."

"Uh huh. And you ain't gay, I'll bet."

"No," I replied honestly, thinking back to a time where we almost hit it off on another level. But the misunderstanding was good as I didn't need another person getting too close to me...and paying for it.

"See. I knew that girl you brought around before wasn't your gal-pal," Helene crowed about Sophia. "The sexual chemistry was obvious. You fuckin' her?"

"Not anymore," I answered, being more truthful than she'd ever know.

"Since you're being honest all of a sudden, want to tell me who those men are who keep walking by and peeking in your windows? You know visitors stand out."

"I'm still trying to figure that out myself," I admitted. "Things are moving fast."

"Are they the reason you look like somebody took a meat tenderizer to you?" she posed, her dark full eyebrows furrowing.

"Friends of theirs probably," I replied as I stood up to face her.

"This is something really bad, huh?"

"The less you know..." I chimed as a jogger passed us.

"Is this like a goodbye then?" she broached.

"Yeah. You'll never see me again," I relented. "Thank you for taking such good care of Buster; and for being a good friend…when I was around."

"I told you his name is Marshawn now," she dug a final time. "Can I have your telescope at least?"

"No. Steer clear," I instructed. "Don't want them thinking we're close. The condo will burn down tomorrow night. With no reason to stick around, you shouldn't see those men again."

"You're gonna do something to them with your good arm? Or beat em with your bad arm like a club?" she joked.

"We'll see," I said, caressing one of her high cheekbones with the back of my hand. "It'll all be alright. Take care, kid."

Against my wishes, Helene gave me a hug and kissed me on my cheek. "You too," she said in parting.

I'd done my best to convey assuredness to her, but if these people knew about my safe house here, then I really was in trouble.

As well as anyone else I'd ever been close to.

Collette, I gasped, leaving my safe harbor a final time.

13-Truth

"You really should go to the hospital for that arm," the veterinarian recommended in Spanish as I paid him.

"Maybe later," I commented dismissively as I showed him out and closed the door.

I put some distance between myself and Seattle, stopping at the Overton Hotel in Lubbock, Texas after switching out several cell phones and cars along the way. Leery of my bank accounts being monitored as easily as places where I chose to lay my head, I tapped into my cash reserves for now.

From a burner phone, I made the dreaded call to the Frisco Police Department, a suburb north of Dallas. I was placed on hold for Detective Kane, but this matter was about his wife, a woman who had a bit of a love-hate relationship with me. To simplify it, I loved Collette and she hated me; hated me enough to wish me dead, which is what I was in her eyes thanks to her husband and a plan of mine to give her piece of mind. She had good reason too for her hatred, blaming me for her first husband's death and her temporary blindness.

I was the blind one though; too blinded by my irrational love as she enlisted Sophia as part of her revenge scheme.

Collette held a gun on me one night years ago. One I'd provided.

"You . . . deserve . . . to . . . die, you bastard!" she had said, baring her teeth as she struggled to breathe. After so long, it was odd watching her glare directly at me. "You took away the one person in the world that meant something to me!"

"I'm sorry for that, Collette," I'd said, pained as I came to realize that despite the momentary fantasy of the past few months, I never had a chance. As angry as I'd been up to that point, the fact that she wanted me dead no longer mattered.

"No, you're not. Don't ever say that!" I heard the hammer click back as Collette prepared to exact her revenge.

"How'd you know? At least tell me that," I implored, prepared for the finality I deserved.

"Your voice. I'll never forget your voice. It's like a bell ringing in my head every time you speak. You were there when it happened. You were there when Myron

blew himself up. You knew. You . . . killed . . . my husband!"

"He did it to himself, Collette. He was cheating on you. I . . . didn't know he'd—"

"Blow himself up and try to kill me too? What kind of monster are you?"

"One that loves you no matter what you think of me."

"Love? Is that what made you fuck Sophia? Love for me?" Collette taunted as she shot at my feet in preparation for the next one. "It sickened me to do the things I did with you. Don't you dare talk to me about love!"

Her then husband's mistress had hired me to break up his marriage so she could have him all to herself. It was my first job free from Jason North's tentacles and I went too far, leading him to believe Collette had been cheating on him, but not anticipating how he'd react. The man blew himself up, taking out their home just as Collette was coming in the door. I was there to witness it all and there as Collette came to terms with her blindness, fraudulently entering her life as an author named Chris.

Perhaps it would've worked out, living that lie, except for mutual interests that led Jason North to sell me out to Collette, revealing the truth about the new man in her life. Even as her eyes healed and vision returned, her desire for revenge never wavered.

But that was in the past, I'd moved on into my strange kinship with Sophia, content to entrust Collette's security and future to the man who was now her husband.

"Detective Kane," the perturbed voice answered amidst the office chatter. He was about to get more disturbed.

"It's me," was all I said. It sufficed.

After a long pause, followed by him putting me on mute he popped back on absent the background noise. "Bruh, this better not be another threat to my wife," he barked.

"It might be. And if it is, it's very serious. There...there have already been casualties. I felt the need to tell you about it," I admitted, staring out the window toward Texas Tech University. A dust storm or haboob was brewing west of here and sweeping across the South Plains in our direction.

"Is this how it's gonna be every few years, bro?" he sighed. "Can't you just get on with your life, man? She ain't your girl and never was. Don't drag us into your shit."

"Don't forget. There wouldn't be an 'us' if it weren't for me," I scolded, feeling the sting of loneliness at the moment. Collette couldn't bring herself to pull the trigger that night, so the former officer Kane of the Dallas PD did it for her, bringing the two of them together. And yes, I had a bulletproof vest on. I'm a regular fuckin' Cupid in Kevlar.

"Hey! I could've thrown you in jail that night. Or put a bullet in your head and been done with it," he barked. "Instead I've kept quiet about you to Collette this entire time, so I ain't letting you hold it over my head anymore. We're square."

"I'm sorry. I didn't call you to argue or get into a dick measuring contest. Someone's gunning for me and they're not being gentlemanly about it. Rules don't apply to these guys," I declared, thinking back those innocents in Paris.

"Does this have anything to do with that guy who had my leg broken that time?" he asked, referring to my last major problem a couple of years back. That was Nathan Piatkowski, a CIA spook who threatened Collette to get me to do his off-the-books dirty work down in the Big Easy. Kane and his police resources came in handy when I needed to track him down.

"No. He's gone," I assured Kane. "Don't know who-or what- it is this time, but they're brutal and know about me. A lot about me. Which brings me to this call. Has anyone unusual been snooping around?"

"No," he replied without even a moment's hesitation.

"Are you certain?" I stressed, which is why I waited until I was close enough to Dallas before placing the call. If necessary, I was willing to risk Collette finding out I was still alive if it meant no harm would come to her. "They might be around your house and you wouldn't know it. I need you to be honest and put your ego aside, because I still have resources and can put some extra security on both you guys."

"Yeah. I know my job, bruh. Nothing's out of the norm," he reassured me with a sharp tone. "And we both know you only care about my wife. So thanks, but no thanks."

"Okay. But you'll hear from me if I learn more."

"I let you live last time I saw you. I ain't one for third chances. Don't call me. Don't come around me. Don't come around Collette," he threatened with finality.

After Kane hung up, I sat at the foot of the bed. The fine bits of dust swirled outside the hotel window now, obscuring my view.

The dust storm was here for the moment, but my vision had been obscured back in Paris and for who knows how long before that. Besides Collette, I had a daughter in New Orleans no one knew about; not even Sophia. Both she and her mother should be safe as long as I didn't contact them.

But as long as I flew blind, not knowing who was after me, I couldn't be certain.

My eyes had to be wide open.

And I needed help.

I reached into my duffel bag and snagged another phone of mine. Dialing a number from memory, I sent a simple text-**Big favor**.

I called it a favor, but the person reading the text knew they couldn't refuse.

ERIC PETE

14-Truth

You never forget the unique stench of subway stations, no matter the country-musk, grease, and urine to varying degrees. Sometimes it's faint; other times, it smacks you in the face and challenges your manhood. This was New York, so I'll let you decide in this instance.

Lorelei Smart could've taken a limo, but once a week she threw on a hoodie and jeans to remind her of old days when she worked at FedExKinkos over by the Garden, misappropriating their computers for her fledgling website 4Shizzle. These days, she rented offices on both coasts with a staff to rival TMZ. Exiting the N Line, she passed the homeless man to whom she always slipped a twenty dollar bill.

But that guy wasn't in his usual spot today. Call me a squatter for I claimed this valuable piece of real estate while the disabled vet relaxed in an Atlantic City suite with unlimited room service courtesy of me.

"I once got busy in a Burger King bathroom," I said as Lorelei had already begun to walk away.

"You," she gasped, not recognizing this smelly, destitute- looking man from the last time we'd met in person. In my line of work, I was sometimes privy to the entertainment world's salacious secrets and generally funneled those stories to her indirectly or via the internet for a fee. From Texas, I'd texted her a specific request along with instructions. I ended it with "The Humpty Dance", the Digital Underground song from which I'd just borrowed a verse.

"Keep looking ahead. Some people down here are not what they seem. Don't want a repeat of Paris," I murmured.

"Holy shit!" she cursed, visibly nervous. "That was you?"

"We got fifteen minutes before the next train gets here," I noted, ignoring her question. "What did you find out?"

"First off, this is not what I do," she argued, sure to get that off her chest.

"I know. I know," I agreed. But she had the resources and talent to peer into bad places without being noticed.

"The Deep Web," she sighed, clenching and releasing her petite fist. "You're trying to sic the NSA on me? I've grown a successful business here peddling my gossip and don't need diversification like this."

"And how much of that growth is due to my scoops over the years? Don't I provide the *tea plus receipts?*" I joked.

"Some," she relented. "But still. You got me using my servers to tip-toe around law enforcement like Interpol and into Darknets where anything goes. The blowback could be unforgiving to a sister. I feel like I need a shower just talking about it."

"Any off-the-grid chatter about Paris? Anything beyond the terrorist theme bullshit we're getting on CNN and FOX News?"

"Yeah, besides the usual conspiracy chatter, one name was floating out there before other concerned people told them to shut the fuck up before they got ghosted. Then...nothing. Poof."

"And the name?"

"Russian I think. 'Dimitri something'," she softly recalled, surveying everyone that strolled the platform with a leery eye.

I intentionally didn't tell Lorelei anything about the men who attacked us as they may have simply been paid muscle and I didn't want to influence her results. What she found suddenly became valuable. "Dimitri what?" I pressed impatiently.

"I'm thinking, I'm thinking! You told me not to save or write anything down," she chided as she smacked her hand on the tile wall rather than upside my head. "Ogletree?" she pondered aloud.

"Ogletree," I repeated, breaking my own instructions not to look at one another. "Are you certain?"

"No...wait. Orlovsky. Yeah, that's it. Orlovsky."

At the sound of that name, my heart rose in my chest and my pulse quickened. Never underestimate the lengths to which family will go. And yet, all those years ago, I had. Stunned, I rose to my feet using my good arm. "Thank you," I stoically offered to her as I dropped a key in her hand. A little something for her trouble awaited in a nearby storage locker.

"Did I do good? Did that help?" she questioned as I left her standing there, the next train pulling up to the station.

"A ton. Now board the train and get outta here," I replied without so much as a backward glance, the homeless man suddenly walking upright and with purpose. In a warped way, things made sense now.

Topside, the two Jamaicans who were tailing me earlier, before my homeless disguise, made me again. Of course, I let them rather than run the risk of endangering Lorelei. Their real employer was smart to use them around these parts, adapting from the blunt force employed in Paris. I let them follow me down 49th St in Midtown Manhattan, unsure whether to kill them with my one good arm or do something more sinister once out the public eye.

The time for thought was over; action was on the agenda as I had a target for my rage.

And what an exquisite weapon I had.

Once I found it.

ERIC PETE

15-Truth

The Past-Boston Massachusetts

Fire trucks sped in the direction of a large plume of thick, inky smoke; a visible sign of the warehouse explosion and fire raging mere blocks away.

With all the attention in the area devoted to that, a woman navigated through the concerned crowds and morbidly curious, sticking to side streets whenever she could; a business woman hauling a conspicuous duffel bag which she kept pressed to her side. She moved quickly enough to where one wouldn't notice anything wrong. But if one were looking very carefully and she happened to slow down, they might notice spatters of blood on her sensible shoes.

I'd watched enough though and knew where she was heading, so I kept my distance and bided my time. I could've left it alone, but I was curious. One artist to another, I guess. Plus her attractiveness wasn't lost on me.

Her complexion and hair texture seemed Dominicana at first glance, but maybe she was a Spaniard mixed with Berber. Or just maybe she was one of them Louisiana Creoles. Could be that she was an Afro Brazilian. That damn school for killers had taught her well with the nondescript accent though. From our little talk, I couldn't nail down her origin, and I was good at that shit.

It didn't take much longer for her to return to her car in Brookline. By its looks, it was an obvious rental. She was cautious in her approach, first making sure the area was clear of threats then turning her attention to the car. Content, she doubled back to a nearby dumpster and ditched her stained shoes. Still, I was nearby and watched as the duffel finally left her embrace.

"Bravo," I said, announcing myself as she slammed the trunk lid shut.

From out of nowhere, she produced a black carbon blade and brought it to my throat. She rightly figured my blobby physique was for show and went straight to an exposed area. Her reflexes impressed me probably as much as my ability to sneak up on her did her. "Why are you still here?" she asked, digging the blade in just slightly near my jugular.

"Wanted to be sure you were okay. And to see if you're as good as I thought," I admitted, slowly peeling away a layer of my facial disguise to show I meant no harm. "Ambushes can be a mother."

"Only if you don't know about them," she reminded me with an appreciative smile, retracting her blade before I could even blink. "With that kind of heads-up, you knew I'd be fine. You just wanted to see if I kept my end of the bargain."

"Did you?" I asked, safe to breathe.

"Yeah. I left Vasili Orlovsky alive for you. You didn't say I couldn't touch him though," she teased as she opened her car door to leave. "I left him on the ground outside the warehouse. Just before I blew it up. He might sneak off, but I'm sure you'll be able to find him. He's missing an ear."

"What's on the agenda? Your next job?" I questioned, reluctant to end our conversation even though I had a one-eared Russian to seek and torment. Knowing how her type was so easy to go ghost, I used every extra second to commit her face and mannerisms to memory. In the future, if I pissed off enough people, she might be coming for me.

"No. Got a nice little haul in the trunk," the Armani assassin smartly replied as she started the car. 50 Cent's "Candy Shop" was mid-song on the radio. "With that plus what they were supposed to pay me, I can disappear to somewhere nice. Maybe set up something less violent for myself."

"But you do violence so well," I complimented with a wink as I touched my throat.

16-Joseline Gunn

Saint Martin Parish, LA

"Don't let her beat you to the ball, Brittani!" her boisterous, overeager mom Chandra howled. The other two women and I just shook our heads and smiled.

Due to renovations and sewer work at Breaux Bridge High School, the youth girls' soccer team practiced at Parc Hardy this early morning. Mothers and fill-ins clustered in the tree line and I shared this particular tree with a few of my new best friends, taking advantage of the scant shade it provided us. It was already sweltering and nearby Bayou Teche reminded me I'd chosen this location all on my own. Thing was, I'd recently been places more oppressive and stifling than this. Plus nobody here was trying to kill me, so that was a plus.

Well, almost nobody.

There was the occasional fish fry and last year's Crawfish Festival where more than a few jealous eyes cut my way. But as long as they kept their knives to culinary pursuits, the new girl in town wouldn't have to "show out". Of course, I can't blame them. My acquaintance Justin Thibeau was a handsome widower and a good provider for his daughter, bucking the deadbeat label of which these single moms around me were victims. Justin was still on his shift this morning at the fire station in Lafayette, so I took up the slack with his daughter Shyla-Anne, getting her dressed and driving her over. That also meant deflecting the usual questions while not coming off as aloof.

"Latrese...what's yo secret, bitch?" Chandra asked me as she took a break from her yelling. "I went to high school with that boy. Thibeau ain't the playin' type; he the committin' type. What you do to get his sexy ass back datin'?"

"Nothin'. I guess it just was time. He still miss Shy's momma tho, but he gettin' his footin' back," I replied, trying to keep my accent as I leaned up against the tree. To them, I was from up north by Port Barre. In reality, it was just a place I'd seen on the map before arriving in Louisiana last year.

"I'll bet. By dippin' them toes in your pool," Roxy teased while eating a link of homemade boudin.

"Why this gotta be about me, bitch?" I asked with a grin. On the makeshift soccer field, Shy beat the girl Brittani into the open with some fancy footwork and scored easily on the goalkeeper. I wanted to cheer, but it was just practice and my friend's girls she'd just straight clowned.

"Cause you da new pussy in town and we all wanna know your secret. Maybe us *common folk* can learn a thang or two," Roxy responded.

"Well, that shit between me and Justin. And if I got some 'secrets', they damn sure stayin' mine," I huffed with a grin.

"Whatever, bitch," Chandra scoffed as she resumed her sideline coaching of her daughter. Poor little thing was torn between listening to her mom and the coach, allowing Shy to pick off her pass and score again.

"Well, I think Justin got some competition out there, Latrese," Tamara, the one who'd kept her mouth shut until now, interrupted. "Girl, you got more secrets?"

"Huh?" I said, halting my lips mid-smack.

"Cause he sho eyeing you like you is on the menu," she continued, pointing across the field from us.

I trained my eyes in that direction, noticing an attractive brother with his arm in a sling staring dead at me. With his good arm, he waved. He hadn't been there earlier and I know I didn't recognize him.

Yet somehow I knew him.

17-Truth

Since Boston and up until a couple of years ago, I kept tabs on the Armani-wearing assassin, following her handiwork for future reference and the long game I tend to play. But then she blinked off the grid, probably back overseas or something. I guess her returning to the US was fortuitous because I was pressed for time and low on resources right now. And by these surroundings, she was truly sticking to the backroads.

I chose to confront her in the open, showing I meant no harm as I guardedly slipped past the little girls kicking the soccer ball around for their coach. Was she a mom now? Three women stood near her which was a good thing for me. Perhaps these kids belonged to them and she was just tagging along. She'd forgone expensive pantsuits this hot as fuck morning for a simple white tee, jean shorts, and a pair of black flip-flops; revealing how athletic and toned her body was. If she wanted to, she could incapacitate all three of her friends in less than a minute. And I, in my current state, would be next. But I wasn't here to fight or die.

"Latrese, you gonna introduce us?" the thickest of the three asked her using what I'm sure was a made-up name.

"Yeah...um...," she fumbled to come up with a name as I observed the anger in her eyes.

"Cuz, long time no see," I interjected as I leaned forward, daring to hug her while hoping I didn't end up with a knife in my gut. "Sorry to come at you unannounced like this, but I have some terrible news."

∞

She instructed me to drive the old Ford truck down the road toward Cecilia, an even smaller town north of Breaux Bridge. To her friends, she was too distraught to drive home after the tragic news I'd delivered-a lie that her favorite aunt, my mother, had committed suicide. I used my mom's name and a real event, the one where she took her own life. It worked because those girls back there were in tears and consoling us when we left, their tawdry thoughts vanished.

"You're a disrespectful mother fucker!" she cursed in Spanish while the spent little girl slept across her lap. Her accent finally betrayed her. She was Dominican and smart to hide out here in Acadiana where no one knew her and her features would blend in well enough.

"Relax. Your friends bought it," I replied in Spanish as well, letting her know it was okay to vent in front of the little girl who knew English and maybe a little French.

"Don't tell me to fuckin' relax. Fuck you, whoever the fuck you are. This ain't cool," she grumbled while shaking her head in disbelief.

"Your daughter?" I calmly asked about the snoring girl in the athletic wear.

"No. My boyfriend's. I'm watching her today while he works," she replied as she rubbed the girl's forehead. "What the fuck do you want from me?"

"I need your help. And that's hard for me to admit," I confessed, courteously keeping my good hand on the steering wheel. It was probably why she wanted me to drive.

"Why would I do that and not just kill you right now? Don't think because I got a kid in my lap that I won't leave you in the Bayou for the gators," she threatened through bared teeth.

"You like this? This life?" I asked, casting a glance at the sleeping child then back to the road.

"I guess. After Boston, I headed down to South America for a few more jobs. Compared to Bogota and Lima, the life here is simple."

"You think," I corrected her. "My mother really was from down I-10 in New Orleans. The Louisiana life is neither simple nor easy. They'll figure you out one day no matter how good you think you are."

"Fair enough, but I'll ask you one more time before somebody's missing you permanently. Why should I help you?" she reiterated, but a little more softly.

"Because I tipped you to that ambush back in Boston. Now I'm cashing in," I declared, knowing she still had some kind of honor code.

"What's your problem?" she asked, her gaze lost in the winding road ahead.

"Orlovsky," was the single name I spoke. I watched out the corner of my eye, sensing just the slightest shudder from her.

"Bullshit. They're dead. Both," she scoffed. "I took out one. And the other one committed suicide after you..."

"There was a third brother; worse than the other two. Dimitri. He somehow knows way too much about me and is going 'scorched Earth'. Making my life hell," I elaborated while wiggling my mangled arm in the sling with a grimace.

"They did that to you?" she asked.

"Yeah. Thing's useless and I don't have time for surgery or rehab to save it. Got it wrapped up, so it doesn't offend, but... this shit's already cost me more than an arm," I admitted, picturing that car blowing up. "The Paris massacre was him."

"No shit?"

"Shit," I somehow managed to joke. "I gave as good as I got and it wasn't enough. Those civilians are all on me."

She had more questions, but we'd arrived at her boyfriend's address. She was surprised to see a black pickup parked in front the double-wide trailer. I parked close enough to see the Fire Department insignia affixed to its door.

"No, no, no," the woman they called Latrese around here genuinely wailed. Feeling the truck had come to a stop, the little girl in her lap stirred from her slumber. "Justin's home early," she gasped, her eyes watering.

ERIC PETE

18-Truth

"Daddy!" the little girl squealed as she leapt from the assassin's lap onto the pavement and ran into her father's arms. The muscled, light skinned man with a beard held a tire iron in his hand, ready for a scuffle, but softened as soon as his daughter embraced him.

"Daddy, they were speaking Mexican and Ms. Latrese said a cuss word," she reported matter-of-factly. The innocence of youth.

"Shyla-Anne, go in the house, baby. Daddy will be there in a minute. He needs to have some grown-up time with Ms. Latrese and her friend," Justin shooed as he held the white screen door open for her. I held my ground near the truck and hoped cooler heads would prevail. I didn't come out here to intentionally shit on his happy life.

"Baby, we need to talk," she said to her boyfriend, unfortunately waving a red cape in front of a fuming bull. And like a bull, Justin charged down the wooden stairs, nostrils flaring as he let his imagination and insecurities determine who I was to her.

"I got off early to see my baby girl, but why somebody call me and say dis nigga here with you at the park?" he accused as he tightened his grip on the black tire iron, veins bulging in his forearms.

"Because this is a small town with small minds," she clapped back still in her Latrese persona. "Your little so called 'spies' are nothin' but jealous bitches."

"Then who dis nigga and why he driving your truck, Latrese?" Justin asked her as he jabbed his tire iron in front my face. As she came around the truck to confront him, I wondered what she might say.

"Hi, I'm Latrese's cousin Telvin. From New Orleans," I quickly offered, extending my good hand in hopes of deescalating this. It kinda worked because he spared me the tire iron, but punched me in my nose instead. Compared to all the other aches and injury I'd endured these days, it was refreshingly minor.

"Y'all don't look nothin' alike. And I thought you said you was from Port Barre, Latrese."

"I am, you idiot!" she scolded as she shoved him away from me. "His momma, my momma's sister, moved to New Orleans. He came to personally deliver some bad news and found me at the park. He didn't come here for you to come at him with a tire iron!"

"I... Look... I'm sorry. But y'all still don't look nothin' alike. And after getting that call, I just lost it," he somewhat apologized as his shoulders slumped in defeat. He extended his hand this time, but I kept holding my nose. His daughter Shyla-Anne's innocent little face peered at us through the screen door, her lip quivering.

"See! I can't take this jealousy shit. Boy, if I was doing something with this man, we wouldn't be showing up at your place. I ain't got time for this," she argued rather convincingly as she snatched her keys back from me. "Get in, Telvin," she ordered, remembering the name I'd just used.

"Baby. Wait," the chiseled fireman begged as he gripped her shoulder a bit too forcefully. In one flowing move, she grasped his wrist and spun out from under him before slamming him face first into the side of her truck. He groaned as he slid onto his knees. At that moment, she noticed Justin's daughter was watching the whole thing. She immediately relented, but that image couldn't be undone.

"Look. Imma call you later. I need to get away and clear my head. Tell Shyla-Anne, I'm sorry," she apologized as she tenderly patted then rubbed a stunned Justin on his back.

∞

"I didn't intend on ruining whatever you had going on," I apologized.

"It was only going to be a temporary thing. I realize that now," she said stone-faced as she prepared to enter I-10 and head west toward Lafayette. Her recent accent was already gone; cast off like old clothes. We had more in common than I thought.

"What's your real name?" I asked in an attempt to move forward cordially. I still had an irrational fear she'd suddenly slit my throat and shove me from the moving truck onto the freeway for my best speed bump impression.

"I can't tell you that. That's not part of the deal. That's never part of the deal," she admonished me, reciting it as if a lesson learned long ago and far away. Her body language was already changing and I struggled to read it.

"Do we even have a deal?" I questioned.

"Joseline," she replied to my first question after several minutes of silent, uncomfortable driving save for the loud exhaust on the old truck. "And yours?"

"Truth," I said as I read mile marker signs like a good little boy.

"*That's really your name*?" Joseline broached with a near chuckle as she finally looked my way. "As in 'Truth or Dare'?"

"Yes," I nodded. "And I've heard that one before."

"You Dominican?" I asked.

"Half. My daddy was Haitian. He was working in the DR when they met. My mom's side of the family had serious issues with that. Except my grandmother, God rest her soul," she revealed as she made the Sign of the Cross, obviously still strong in her convictions.

"Oh," I feebly offered, my curiosity piqued as to what kind of life she led before winding up in one of those schools for elite assassins. For a second I thought about that Zoe Saldana film *Colombiana*.

A switch thrown, Joseline suddenly sped up, crossing over two lanes of honking traffic before screeching to a halt along the freeway shoulder. Without my seatbelt on, I almost slammed into the dash and maybe that's what she intended. I tensed up, figuring maybe she was gonna try to off me after sharing details about her life. That had to be some kind of code violation I guess.

"Look, I need you to tell me exactly what my services will be," she ordered instead, ending whatever debate had been raging inside her head. I let out a deep sigh of relief.

"Simple. Keep me alive and help me kill Dimitri Orlovsky," I replied, my mind dead set on avenging Sophia in the most painful ways possible. Still, I tried to simultaneously ignore Joseline's pleasing thighs sidling across the worn bench seat in my direction.

"That's it?" she followed up warily.

"Yes. That's it. Then, if we're still alive, we go our separate ways."

"And I never see you again?" she asked, sliding even closer.

"Yes."

"Under penalty of immediate death by my hand?"

"Uh...yes," I agreed with those very hands way too close.

"Then we have a deal, Truth," she proclaimed, clasping my face in her hands.

And kissing me full on the lips.

"What was that about?" I asked, not even hiding my surprise. It felt more like a scene from the Godfather than anything romantic.

"Now the agreement is binding. It's the way of the Nest. The intimacy seals it," she remarked all businesslike.

"Did you do this with Leonid Orlovsky back in Boston?" I dared to ask.

"Yes. And you saw what happened when he tried to go back on our deal," she was quick to remind me. "If you betray or double-cross me, I will kill you," she said from behind eerily calm eyes.

"What made you change your mind?"

"It's a woman's prerogative. Plus I'm a realist. You contributed to one Orlovsky brother's death. I'm responsible for the other brother plus two entire crews. And based on today, I might not be that good at hiding. If   this Dimitri is trying this hard to kill you, I'm probably next."

"Then let's be proactive," I suggested, breaking a smile.

ERIC PETE

19-Truth

I got a message left for me by Collette's husband back in Texas, Detective Kane. It was urgent enough to make us drive all night, stopping in Longview where Joseline stocked up on the tools of her trade. God bless Texas, for they love their guns and ammo.

For the fourth time on this drive, I played the message on speaker for Joseline to hear as well just as we pulled into Bob Jones Park in Southlake, northwest of Dallas near DFW Airport:

"It's Kane. I know when I said I could handle everything on my own. Well, I can't. Some dangerous people been coming around and it's got me spooked. I think I got something that can help put an end to this. Meet me at the spot."

"Why here?" Joseline asked as she surveyed the nature preserve before choosing a parking spot.

"This place has significance. It's where he put a bullet in me."

"Huh?"

"It was according to plan. My life's crazy," I admitted, strongly in need of another pain pill that I no longer had.

"Need me to go with you?"

"No. Strangely enough, I trust him. He's looking out for someone close to me. But if you see anybody enter the park that looks like a Russian thug, you know what to do."

"I most certainly do," she joked with a wink from behind her sunglasses.

I left Joseline and took a wooded trail deeper into the preserve, retracing steps taken long ago, but which felt like just yesterday. A time when Collette confronted me and I learned I was the blind one.

It always came back to Collette; and by extension her husband Detective Kane now. The first time I showed weakness and it had forever been used as a pawn against me. Maybe if I survived this time, I'd learn to steel myself and stay true to the darkness inside.

An unmarked car arrived, a white Dodge Charger driving down the path meant only for hikers and grounds crew. Or in this case, law enforcement.

Detective Kane exited the car; not in an official uniform, but the burnt orange warmups of the University of Texas. That was probably best as he was out of his jurisdiction anyway. I flagged him down and walked over.

"You came by yourself?" he asked as we stood face-to-face. He sized me up, remembering our last fight when I was a bit more able. The man looked aged and weary. The stress of looking over your shoulder can do that. I think we pitied each other equally.

"See someone with me?" I snapped, feeling a bit ornery from my injuries and lack of sleep. "Talk to me. What kind of numbers are you looking at?"

"I don't know how many, man," he replied. "People been following me around and I can't shake 'em. I'm the law and it's got me spooked. It's like they don't care. I tried confronting one of 'em and flashed the badge, but he just smiled and acted like he didn't know what I was talking about. I got some of my boys on extra patrol by the house, but without telling 'em what's going down, it's almost worthless. You know how I feel about you. And as a grown ass man, it pains me to be even asking for your help."

"And I just want to stay out of your life. Furreal. But today, I'm here to help," I offered. "Did they directly threaten Collette? Because, as you can see, these guys don't bluff. I can get both of you to a safe house until this is over and she doesn't have to know I'm involved."

"I think it's too late for that," Kane said, his voice sounding weird. "I think they're here."

A tree branch snapped and I hesitated, whipping my head around at the surrounding woods. And in that moment of distraction, I learned the real deal.

"I'm sorry," Kane said as he pointed a throwaway revolver to my temple. It must've been tucked in his waistband all along.

"Whoa. Easy there. I know we're not best buds, but this ain't the way to handle things," I attempted to reason.

"I got no choice," he desperately explained in gasping breaths. "He promised that if I kill you, this will be all over."

"Have you ever killed anyone, Kane?" I asked.

"Shut up! He told me you'd try to talk your way out. Well, I ain't listenin'."

I knew that tone; it was one of finality and conviction. I'd been played by Kane and Orlovsky had won; a damn perfect set-up. My hubris got the best of me and now I was gonna pay the ultimate price. This was my third time here with Kane. The first time, he shot me, but I planned it. The second time, he pulled a gun on me, but we fought instead. I guess the third time's the charm. Time to call it a day, I suppose. Rather than closing my eyes, I stared ahead into the abyss welcoming me home. Hell, my pulse wasn't even racing.

The Detective cocked back the hammer then I felt a brush of wind on my face. Next came the gunshot followed by blood splattering on my face.

But it wasn't quite how you'd expect.

And the ghastly, soul rattling scream really didn't fit because I wouldn't go out like that.

That was because neither the scream nor the blood was mine.

The abyss whispered back to me, "*Not yet, Truth.*"

I turned to Detective Kane, witnessing the utter shock in his eyes. I was equally surprised.

His hand was gone; in particular, his shooting hand. The gun discharged just as it fell to the ground while still gripped. His bloody stump spewed like a sprinkler as he howled.

We had company.

Joseline stood between us, her machete freshly painted with Kane's blood.

Succumbing to the blood loss, Kane curled up in a fetal position. His screams mixed in with murmurs and sobs as he held his stubby limb close to his body. He was about to go into shock. I snapped back to the task at hand and stood over him.

"My...my hand!" he stammered.

"You've met the Russian? Where is he? Is he nearby? Tell me!" I yelled at him, ignoring his plight.

"Russian? Nah. He's American," he replied as a delirious calm overcame him. "It was that dude whose fingerprint you had me run last time. The one who threatened us before."

"*Before*?" I repeated, positive I misunderstood and that he was rambling from blood loss.

"You were supposed to have taken care of that, but you didn't, bitch. He's back," he cursed, breathing through clenched teeth.

"Wait. *Piatkowski*?" I questioned, fighting back the vomit in my throat.

"Yeah. I remember his face from his driver's license. You said that was over. This time, he promised me it really would be over if I did this."

"Who's Piatkowski?" Joseline asked, interrupting my impromptu, desperate interrogation of a one-handed man.

"Someone who's supposed to be dead," I bitterly answered her.

"Wait. You have two people coming for you?" she asked, leaning over me to better observe Kane.

"Yeah. And working together apparently. The story of my life," I responded. "Got a problem with it?"

"No. For now," she stated, placing her hand on my shoulder. She'd saved my life and was so calm about it. "Let's go. Somebody probably heard the gunshot. You can thank me later."

"What about him?" I asked just as I almost mindlessly followed her.

"Oh. Right," she agreed as she doubled back and stood over Kane, raising her machete in the air for a more final swing.

"What are you doing? He's five-oh!" I yelled.

"And he tried to murder you. He lost," she reminded me, determined to finish it.

"No. Wait! You can't," I complained as I foolishly grabbed her wrist.

"Huh? What's wrong with you?" she said, supremely annoyed.

"He was being forced to do it. Now he needs medical attention before he bleeds out," I said, exhibiting some empathy.

"You're crazy. Crazier that I suspected. What are you keeping from me?" Joseline pressed. She had good intuition.

"His wife. I owe her. She's lost too much already thanks to me. And he just did me a favor. Now we know how Orlovsky got his intel," I clinically argued.

"I don't work like this and I'm seriously beginning to dislike you," she relented as she stood up and retreated.

"We good, Kane?" I asked him, slapping his face to maintain his focus on me. And to make sure he understood the deeper meaning.

"Yeah. We good," he gasped, his eyes expressing gratitude for the first time ever.

"Let's get him out of here before he goes into shock," I said as I removed my belt and used it as a makeshift tourniquet around his forearm.

20

New Orleans, LA

"The address should be ahead on the right," he called out to the emotionless Russians in the front seat as they headed down Canal St. They'd just left a gentleman's club in New Orleans East, but without whatever it was he was seeking.

Even with his altered appearance, Piatkowski slumped low in the backseat behind tinted windows, certain that he wasn't welcome anymore in his home country as he had been before his abduction and imprisonment. That black bastard, or *The Black Ghost* as Orlovsky referred to him, had seen to that.

Piatkowski missed this city full of more character and vibrancy than his staid other life back in the DC suburbs of Virginia. It pained him to admit it now, but he was bored with his wife and legal family, which is why he relished the dangerous government assignments that kept him here along the Gulf Coast and Mexico back then.

But that same work led him into an affiliation with the mighty Braxton "Bricks" Lewis, once the pipeline for Mexican cartels to the entire Gulf Coast as well as Piatkowski's informant. Piatkowski further complicated that arrangement when he fathered a child with Bricks' sister Veronica, but he couldn't help himself. He'd always held a secret fondness for black flesh and these trips to the Crescent City allowed him delve into his cravings with no thought as to the consequences. Of course, there are always consequences; the personal and professional relationships intersected for him in the worst way possible. He'd lose both his career and his visible other life unless he coerced an outsider to do his bidding. That didn't work out as he planned and everything still crumbled apart. Yet here he was alive and back in New Orleans, so that had to count for something.

"This is it," the man in the passenger seat up front called back as they stopped in front of a newly renovated two story building on Canal St. just past North Derbigny, part of the post-Katrina revitalization of recent years. The custom sign out front displayed the name Itz All U Salon and Spa. Piatkowski smiled at the sight as his companions went about routinely checking their weapons before concealing them yet again. Maybe they wouldn't need them as they had back at the gentleman's club, but Piatkowski wouldn't bet on it.

"Sirs, are y'all sure y'all in the right place?" the effeminate receptionist skeptically addressed the three white men after buzzing them in. One them grinned in amusement, but declined responding to the man with impeccable eyebrows and makeup. Piatkowski nervously stepped forward, running his hands through his freshly dyed hair before he spoke.

"Is this Veronica Lewis' establishment?" he asked.

"Yes it is, honey. You need someone to get that horrendous dye job out your hair?" the receptionist offered mockingly. Piatkowski's two associates shared a robust laugh.

"No. I need to speak with her if she's in," he followed up, keeping his impatience in check. He was nervous enough on the private flight back to America, but chose to come here rather than waiting in Dallas in the hopes his target would surface there. He didn't have to linger long for his answer as the woman he sought walked into view. She seemed timeless in her all black attire, exuding the air of a successful businesswoman these days.

Despite the awful orange-blonde hair color and weight loss from his time in captivity, she recognized him immediately. His limp more pronounced, he took a step in her direction, but stopped. Ronnie was never someone to simply just run up on.

"LaRon, we got a gas leak in the building," she calmly stated to the receptionist without taking her eyes off her new guests. "Everybody needs to go out the side door. Now."

"Um...okay, boss," LaRon agreed as he hastily jumped out his seat and sped to the back.

He analyzed her facial expressions, but they refused to betray her at the moment. He hoped that maybe some joy would grace her eyes, but his fishing came up empty.

A behemoth he recognized as her right hand man Ezell emerged from the back with a skinny tag-a-long with sunken eyes, immediately aggressive in their posture. "These don't look like your old friends, white boy," Ezell spat as he and the other one drew on them. They responded in kind, five guns pointing everywhere with Ronnie calmly in the middle.

"I'm not here to quarrel," he recited as if in any Third World hotspot from his past, daring to stow his handgun as he took a few more brave steps toward her.

"What the fuck did you think you'd get after how you did my family?" she chastised as she met him, slapping him hard enough to snap his head back. With the tension broken, everybody decided to put their weapons down for now.

"I looked for you at Fancy's," he offered as he checked his jaw alignment, referring to the gentleman's club that she ran as a legitimate front for her brother, but also where she performed under the stage name "Ron DMC".

"I ain't there no more. And my brother gone, Nate," she spat. "Mexicans came pay him a visit soon as them reports of him being a snitch for y'all came out. Somebody greenlighted his ass. Know anything about that? Where were you, white boy? Certainly ain't dead, like I heard. How you get to live and Bricks is dead? Guess I should be glad. At least one of my kids might grow up knowing they daddy; if I let you outta here alive. Where you been since you abandoned us? Huh? Back in Virginia with yo boring wife and kid?"

"No. They're dead," he replied, his words absent air. "We've both lost someone since then."

"Oh. I... I'm sorry, Nate," Ronnie genuinely offered, some of her brashness suddenly tempered. Not buying it, Ezell just shook his head. He never understood these two or their relationship.

"They died in a car wreck while I was away," Piatkowski added. "So you and little Nate are literally the only family I've got. I'm part of something a whole lot different now as you can see. I've made new friends and can offer better protection than before. Things are gonna be different between me and you. I promise. What do you think about the two of you moving to Europe?"

"Boy, you trippin'. I ain't leaving the Crescent City," she scoffed with a laugh. "And amazing how you forget I got two kids, not just yours. I ain't got time for that anyway. I got a business to run."

"Your new business going well?" he asked as he circled around with his arms out, taking it all in. Everything in here looked first rate from the furniture to the fixtures.

"Yeah. I got legit respect and building up my clientele every damn day. Even got white ladies from the Garden District and Lakeview coming around to get done up. I got some classy shit and ain't ever lettin' go. No more strippin' for me," Ronnie bragged as she adjusted her black attire over her womanly curves.

"Any other revenue?" he pursued, sizing up her current situation.

Veronica smiled sheepishly. "Maybe," she replied as she signaled for Nathan, and only Nathan, to follow her to the back. Both their crews resumed their virtual standoff as they took a walk through her establishment.

Hidden near the kitchen and breakroom, Ronnie revealed a false wall to Nathan. She led him down a secret hallway to a vault door. After punching in a code, she opened it to reveal five topless women in white surgical masks hard at work cutting powder. "We're small time now. Just a little extra action they allow me to keep out of respect for my brother," she explained before quickly shutting the door.

In that moment, he was close enough to smell her hair and he inhaled deeply. Overcome with grief after learning his legal family was gone, he'd forsaken Orlovsky's gifts of drugged out Eurotrash, but now he needed Veronica. He desperately wanted to bend her over the kitchen table and take her right there in her salon. Even though he knew he was never the only one, the sex with her was always exquisite.

"I know I've contributed nothing to you and little Nate's well-being in years, but I can do it now," he prefaced his attempt at intimacy, knowing finance always came before romance with her. "Can we go somewhere alone? Maybe catch up on old times?" he almost begged, remembering that particular thing she did with her tongue of which he was so fond.

"Like I said, my brother is dead and I ain't feeling too accepting right about now. You promised you'd protect him, Nate. And you didn't. You just up and disappeared on us."

"That wasn't my fault," he began to explain. "I had someone who couldn't be connected to me. He was gonna take care of that D.A. situation for you guys, but I got double-crossed and taken away by some really bad people."

"Yeah. I met that dude you hired," she admitted, her face scrunching. "He came by Fancy's once, acting all high and mighty and telling us to back away from the D.A.'s family 'n shit. I shoulda let Ezell ventilate him that night. At least tell me that nigga's dead," she implored.

"My new friends almost got him in Paris, but he slipped away. We killed this bitch he worked with at least. But don't worry, he's back stateside now and he's got weaknesses too. Matter of fact, he should be dead as we speak," he bragged as he hoped to score some points with her.

"For real?"

"Yes," he cockily replied as he took out his phone and placed a call. "Sometimes the simplest solutions are the best."

After several rings with no answer, he got a little nervous. The person he was calling assured him two hours ago that it would be done. Just as he was about to hang up and try again, they answered.

"Give me good news. Is my problem solved, Detective Kane?" he asked, smiling at Ronnie and already imagining a welcome return between her legs. Maybe he'd try for another baby. Interracial families weren't uncommon and once he convinced her to move to Europe or maybe some Caribbean island with no extradition she'd see how happy they really could be.

"Yes," the man on the other end replied, sounding out of breath. "He's dead. I killed him."

21-Truth

Using cold, hard logic, I preferred not taking Kane to a hospital, but options were scant if I wanted to keep him alive. After a hectic change of clothes, I came up with a strategy I hoped would work. With Joseline's reluctant help, I threw Kane in his car and drove him to Baylor Medical Center in the nearby town of Trophy Club, a name that shouted affluence and excess in your face. As soon as we arrived, they took his severed hand and rushed to preserve it in ice water. When asked for an explanation, I stuck to him being a cop who was attacked at the park and left it at that. Mindful of the security cameras, I never provided a full-on view to any of them.

"Sir, apparently you are hard of hearing, so I'll speak up and make myself loud and clear. We're trying to save this man's hand and his life and we need you to move to the waiting room just like everyone else!" the head surgeon bellowed as he arrived from his emergency page, quickly reading Kane's chart and preparing for what would be hours of surgery.

"And you don't understand, doctor. I need just a bit more of his time," I barked back, flashing my fake badge for like the third time in the last thirty minutes. The suit I wore looked official enough and I changed my accent and cadence to project former high level military. Joseline, not having the temperament for this kind of thing remained on guard outside the hospital in case we suddenly had company. Maybe she was just saner than me, which wasn't hard to believe. Or maybe she figured the real police would arrest me and she could go back off the grid. Nah, her honor code wouldn't allow that; so a vicious indebted killing machine was the most trustworthy person in my life right now.

Just as I continued to argue, Kane's burner phone buzzed in my pocket. I got enough out of him on the drive here to know he was expecting this call. It took all my self-control not to answer and crow to Piatkowski that he was still a miserable failure. I had a more difficult path to take though.

"Doctor...this may be difficult for you to understand, but I'll need a brief moment of privacy with Detective Kane before you move him to surgery. That's all I ask then I'll get out of your hair."

"Are you crazy?" he scoffed as he brushed past me to check on Kane's erratic vitals and flash a penlight into his pupils. "I make the rules here and I don't care who you are. I'm about to have security escort you out my facility and throw your ass out on the curb."

"Doctor," I began, daring to grasp his shoulder. "This is a matter of national security and an ongoing critical investigation. Do you care about America, sir? Better yet, are you a proud American?" I broached, attempting to put the Texan on the defensive with my rapid-fire lies.

"Well...yes, but I don't see—"

"Good. It's not for you to see," I asserted, cutting him off and pushing where I sensed a weakness. "Now you and your staff please give us a minute alone and I'll let you get back to your job helping this heroic individual here."

All he could muster was a glare and a begrudging nod at me. I sold the surgeon my bullshit, getting him and his staff to clear out ever so briefly. Kane's IV drip had him sedated, but I needed him awake and slapped him to come to. "Hey. I need you to focus before I answer this phone. Just like we discussed. I saved your life and brought you here when I didn't have to, but do this for Collette," I reminded him through his haze.

His eyes flared with clarity upon the mention of his wife's name. His love for her was strong and she had no idea what he was going through right now. But a hacked off hand isn't something that could be kept from her for very long.

Somehow Kane found the strength to motion for the phone as it was on its final ring. I didn't have time to listen in and just handed it over without hesitation, trusting he understood the consequences for all. I heard a voice on the other end and assumed Kane was in the moment enough to understand. At least I hoped he was.

"Yes," Kane replied to whatever was asked of him, taking a dry gulp as he almost faded into unconsciousness again. "He's dead. I killed him," he somehow completed. For a millisecond, I contemplated that reality had Joseline not intervened. Whatever the reply, it seemed to stir him, his eyes blinking rapidly and his vitals spiking. Then he handed the burner back to me, the person having already hung up.

"What did he say?" I pestered as the surgeon and his team cursed just beyond the closed curtains. Our alone time was up.

"He...he wants to see your body. Will...will be here tomorrow morning," Kane mumbled as his eyes went shut.

The head surgeon yanked the curtains back, his staff quickly filling in behind him. "I'm sorry. If he wants to keep his hand, we can't wait any longer," he said.

"By all means. Go ahead," I relented, having all I could get from Kane.

At least for the moment.

∞

Eight hours later and with the sun down, we made the trek northeast to a neighborhood in Frisco. At the end of Bryson Drive, I drove by a red brick single story home with a patrol car out front; part of Kane's weak attempt at keeping his wife safe. What went down in Paris proved that neither Dimitri Orlovsky nor my old friend "Mr. Smith" would let that get in their way.

I was behind the wheel in Kane's unmarked car and wearing his UT hoodie draped over my head. I hit the LED strobe lights one time and nodded as I slowly rolled by. The patrolman took the bait, thinking I was Kane and drove off.

"He's gone," I said as the taillights grew fainter in the rearview mirror. Joseline popped up from the backseat where she'd been tending to a deliriously feverish Kane. Our escape from the hospital recovery room was a tense moment to say the least, but Kane was needed elsewhere.

We took the alley around back, parking outside the garage.

"Wha...where are we?" Kane mumbled, oblivious to his surroundings as well as the Frankenstein-like external fixator that kept his reattached hand immobile and stabilized.

"Relax. You're home," I replied while searching for his house keys. It took both of us to keep Kane on his feet and when the porch light suddenly came on, we were unable to do anything about it. A single eye peered from behind parted blinds followed by the turning of knobs and slide of a bolt. Both Joseline and I tensed up, me more.

"Oh my God! Clarence, where have you been! Baby, what happened to you?" his wife cried as she rushed into a full, tearful clinch of her husband. Joseline and I fought to steady Kane, stumbling backwards on the stairs. Her husband shielded me from her direct view.

"He had some unfortunate luck and a hospital down in Trophy Club is gonna want some answers, but you needed to know," I spoke for her unresponsive husband as I tentatively glanced over his shoulder.

"No. No. No," she shuddered as our eyes met. On reflex, she recoiled, but quickly grasped him again, clinging tightly. Was she looking to Kane for protection or to protect *him*?

"Hello, Collette," I uttered, the words I'd dreamed of many times, but never once thought I'd truly speak.

"Truth," she gasped, saying a word she never dreamed of speaking again.

22-Truth

We swapped Kane's car with Collette's Accord and stowed it in the garage. After gathering some extra clothes, toiletries and essentials, we placed Collette in the back seat with her husband where she was now, blindfolded and sobbing hysterically. I drove just under the speed limit so as not to attract attention.

"Why are you doing this, Truth? Are you into kidnapping now? Can't ruin lives enough the old way?" she wailed in succession. I'd spent many a night yearning to hear her voice again, but this was slow torture.

"You're not being kidnapped. We have to get you to a safe place. I have somebody qualified on call waiting to render aid to...Clarence," I said, unaccustomed to speaking Kane's first name. It was too personal and we were never gonna be homies. "The blindfold is just a precaution. Please don't cry."

"You drove my first husband to suicide. Now Clarence's hand is destroyed because of you? How sadistic are you? Just die already!" she cursed.

It would be less than beneficial to tell her I had something to do with Kane's hand being lopped off or that his broken leg years ago was Piatkowski's first attempt to coerce me. Instead, I stuck to the matter at hand. "The man who wants me dead will kill both of you once he thinks it's done. I'm going out of my way to shield you from that outcome otherwise I wouldn't have shown up at your door. Please believe me."

"He's speaking the truth," Joseline added, breaking her silence. She'd found a way to *gently* coax Collette along without removing any of her limbs, so that was a positive.

"Who the fuck is she, Truth? A new bitch you're deluding?" the once love of my fantasy life asked, a bit of defiance peppering her despair. "Whatever happened to Sophia? Is she part of this too?"

"No. She's dead," I solemnly answered as I sped up to merge onto the Sam Rayburn Tollway. For a moment, my good hand trembled on the steering wheel. I just clenched harder to make it go away. "She was killed by the same people I'm trying to protect the both of you from."

"Oh," she wheezed, her full lips distorting with emotion. Collette was responsible for my introduction to Sophia, hiring the wannabe actress to gain my confidence, seduce me, then reveal all my secrets and weaknesses to her. Collette really had it in for me back then and Sophia did well; so well that she became my apprentice because even I can appreciate talent. My showing up alive on her doorstep was probably more traumatic than Kane's present condition.

∞

We holed up inside a cheap apartment in Oak Cliff. The irony wasn't lost on me that it wasn't far from where Collette lived with her first husband...before he died and she temporarily lost her sight. But I knew this was one spot free of Piatkowski or any Russian mother fucker's influence, so fuck niceties. The elderly trauma nurse who owed me a favor tended to Kane, busily administering antibiotics to him in the bedroom. He'd quit groaning so at least his pain was subsiding. I needed to hit her up for some pain killers for me before the night was over.

"I need him healthy and coherent enough for one last task in the morning. Then we'll be gone," I assured Collette as I reached out, touching her shoulder as she paced back and forth in the hallway. My hand lingered perhaps a moment too long on her exposed ebony skin. But it just felt right, so very familiar. I almost complimented her on her short, natural hairdo as if there were small talk to be made between us.

"My husband knew about you, didn't he? He knew you weren't dead when he shot you back then. That was all staged for me," she accused as she swatted my hand away and resumed wearing out the carpet.

I ignored her. Or least I pretended to. "There are some James Patterson novels by the bed. A little something for you. Just how you like," I awkwardly broached instead.

She responded by slapping me upside my head, unable to restrain herself any longer. "Still no peace in your life, so you gotta fuck it up for the rest of us. Is what I have with Clarence even real? Or was this another of your crazy schemes?" she confronted me, finally stopped in her tracks. "I don't know why I bother asking. Everything out of your pitiful mouth is a lie anyway," she dismissed as we locked eyes. I blinked first. Damn her for making me uncomfortable in my skin.

"Go. Be with him. He loves you and needs you right now," I threw out as I walked away.

"Everyone suffers because of you, Truth! Whether you mean for it to happen or not," she shouted, her voice filling every square foot of the apartment.

Beaten back by the clarity of her words, I retreated to the other bedroom. Better to clear my head for what I'd have to do tomorrow and the next five steps I needed to be up on. With my body failing, my mind needed to be razor sharp. Maybe an hour or two of sleep could give me my edge back.

Joseline showered in the bathroom and I sat on the bed. I slipped my sling off, grimacing in discomfort as I clenched my teeth. She emerged from the shower, coconut scented steam lingering in the air behind her. Her curly hair was still damp and water rolled down her shoulders onto the tan towel wrapped around her as she studied me. Small scars, mementos of prior wars, adorned what was otherwise the flawless physical form. My mouth boorishly hung open before I realized it. Then it remained affixed that way as she finished drying herself off and yanked the towel free to dry her hair. Her body was a weapon in more ways than one.

"You don't think she's in there calling 911?" Joseline posed as she bent over to gaze at herself in the mirror, teasing her hair with her fingers.

"No. She'll behave," I replied, staring at her ass.

"Y'all two carry on like a married couple," she groused, matter-of-factly ignoring my enthralled gaze. Even when she wasn't listening, she was.

ERIC PETE

23-Truth

An old, seldom used morgue in rural east Texas was where I planned for Kane to meet Mr. Smith. His excuse was that my unidentified body was retrieved before Kane could move it. Then he just had to sell them that as the truth.

I paid off the real coroner, under the pretense of a Hollywood studio needing to film here for the day, giving him enough cash to quietly take a nice one day trip to Vegas and not notify the county of his paid holiday.

Joseline and I waited like sitting ducks while Kane met outside with Mr. Smith. We not only had to rely on the son of a bitch not knowing I was on to him, but also on Kane not to betray us.

Kane walked out of range, too far for the transmitter, so I couldn't hear his conversation until he returned with four guests. I was uncomfortable in this vulnerable position, but had a part to play and prayed Mr. Smith was among them.

"You the one who called about the John Doe we found down by the creek?" I heard Joseline ask from my vantage point, sounding totally unrecognizable. She'd only been working on her slow drawl gospel mash-up for an hour, but you could swear she was from nearby Tatum.

"Yes," Kane struggled to say. Dude probably had about another hour left in him before he totally crashed and burned. But I promised a sobbing, protesting Collette this morning that we would return her husband to her. Our little party wouldn't last long anyway; At least as long as there were no more of them waiting outside. Then I guess we'd move on to the after-party.

"Y'all gotta sign in. We got procedures around here even if you is law enforcement," Joseline reminded them, clad in hospital scrubs, a white lab coat and pillow under her top simulating pregnancy. While unable to see, I heard someone hastily scribbling on her clipboard.

"Y'all brought a lot of people for a John Doe," she remarked, playing her role. She even faked a labored waddle; hand on her side, as she led them over to the refrigerated lockers along the wall. "Honey, you sure you okay?" she asked of Kane as she rested her hand on the drawer handle, continuing the small talk while being genuinely concerned. The hesitation also allowed me to see everyone was in position.

"I'm...I'm fine," Kane mumbled, surrounded by the four men who had little to say. Based on my Paris encounter, they were all about that action and I had no doubt they'd slap Kane and small town coroner Joseline in adjoining drawers as soon as I was a confirmed kill.

"He's a little under the weather," the voice I finally recognized as Mr. Smith's answered, taking over the conversation. It took all my might not to budge, so eager to off him and solve half my problem. At least he was here. "We just need to identify the body then leave you to your work."

"Y'all need to be careful. This body's been out in the heat and already begun to rot. So if y'all squeamish, the garbage can's over there," Joseline warned them as she prepared to slide open the refrigerated drawer.

Joseline tugged on the drawer supposedly housing my remains then stepped aside for them to see. A day old body is one thing. But a rotted, festering cow carcass is on another level. They were unprepared for the stench, maggots and flies that besieged them. Despite their training, they recoiled, vomit rising in their throats as they retreated. Joseline deftly shed her temporary baby bump and was already reaching into her lab coat.

I sat up on table where I'd lay motionless this entire time, a toe tag still attached to my bare foot as the sheet fell away, and fired a nine millimeter with my good hand. The bullet struck the one I'd heard speaking, shattering the back of his skull before erupting out the front of his face. As the other three turned in alarm at the new threat, Joseline jabbed a scalpel in base of one's skull, severing his spinal column. One of the others snapped out of his stupor and threw a fist at the down home coroner he suddenly realized wasn't very pregnant at all. Joseline anticipated his actions and easily ducked under his wild swing. In a single fluid motion, she slit his throat with another scalpel from her lab coat. He fell to the floor burbling and gurgling while attempting in vain to stem the tide of blood pumping freely out his carotid artery, failing to notice his other wounds she'd inflicted just as quickly. Kane hobbled out of the way, feebly throwing his reattached hand up in defense as the last fully functioning man charged him, figuring it an easier path out of here than myself or an able-bodied Joseline. But Kane went untouched, the man clumsily tumbling at his feet. With so many tools at her disposal, Joseline found a surgical saw and went low, raking it across the fleeing man's Achilles tendon. As he rolled onto his back and attempted to draw his firearm, she pounced atop him like some sort of predator and snapped his neck.

"You're done. You and Collette will be safe now," I recited as I went to assist Kane before he fell over.

"He...he's not here," he uttered.

"Bullshit. I heard him," I testily responded as I ran over the bodies to get a better look at their faces. I yanked off their sunglasses to stare into motionless eyes, hopeful for a positive ID. Even if Mr. Smith had some facial reconstruction, I'd still know him. "Fuck! He's not here! None of these are him!" I cursed in frustration after just a minute. But I knew I heard him. There was no way I fuckin' imagined it.

Then I heard the voice again.

"Is it him? Send me the fuckin' picture and let me know if it's clear," the voice coming from the cell phone on the floor instructed. The phone belonged to the one I'd shot. Piatkowski was never in the room with us; he was on speaker the whole time.

"Outside. He's waiting outside. I couldn't warn you," Kane strung together as he braced himself against one of the tables. "He...he was gonna kill me, but then he saw my hand. He believed me when I said we'd struggled and I killed you, but he still didn't trust me enough to come in."

"Truth..." Joseline began to say, her mind coming up with a strategy.

But I was already running down the hall, full-on toward the front door and no longer caring what awaited me. There would be a reckoning for all the trouble and pain this man had caused me and those in my life.

Spotting the lone black Suburban parked beneath the tree, I saw Piatkowski in the back seat still calling out into his phone for someone to reply.

The front doors to the morgue building flinging open drew his attention and he did a double-take as I furiously closed on the SUV, very much alive. Those men back there were expendable to him just as anybody he'd used as pawns in the past. Cutting his losses, he yelled to the driver to get out of there just as I unloaded the clip in their direction. My adrenaline and weary body threw off my aim and I failed to hit anything substantial.

With the cloud of dust getting further and further away, I put the bloody spattered phone I'd retrieved back in the coroner's office to my ear. For a moment, I let him hear me breathe.

"Always unpredictable. I see that hasn't changed," Mr. Smith chirped, pretending he wasn't rattled. "You don't look so well."

"Whatever hell you've crawled from out of, you're going to regret ever fucking with me," I vowed. "Because you're going back and this time I swear I'll make it permanent."

"You have no idea what your black ass cost me all these years," he snarled, Al-Bin Sada's less-than-tender mercies probably permanently etched on his psyche. But he brought that on himself.

"You and these Russian apes failed in Paris. You failed with Kane. And you failed today. You stay losing, *boy*," I taunted. "So go ahead and run, scared little bitch. I know who I'm dealing with now and your next loss will be the final one."

24

Lyon, France

"Look! This is going to work out, Veronica," he desperately tried to assure her as the Mercedes van with tinted windows made its way down the cramped Rue Renan.

"Nate, you are full of shit!" she challenged. Even when she cursed him, he liked the way she called his name. Before her, no one ever called him Nate. It just never was used, having always been either Nathaniel or his last name, Piatkowski. Nate made him feel tough and capable; not just an analyst or lowly field operative, but a man of action. He even started having his subordinates call him that. But that was his past. His government now thought him either dead, a traitor or both thanks to a certain elusive someone.

"No, I'm serious. Will you just fucking listen?" he pleaded with the mother of his only living child, knowing his conversation was about to come to an abrupt end. Could he have killed the son of a bitch back in Texas? Perhaps. But with four of Orlovsky's men dead and not knowing what he was dealing with, his own prior experience filled him with self-doubt. Better to retreat and wait for another opportunity even though he no longer had the element of surprise.

"I ain't listenin' to shit! I remember when you first stepped to me. You was this bad ass cowboy who promised to make our lives easier; to keep the government, the po-pos and the competition off our back. You was supposed to have the juice! Now this bitch ass nigga playing you all over the globe; got you lookin' like an amateur. I tell you this much...if that mother fucker ain't dead, don't bring your ass back to New Orleans. You can just disappear again for all I care because I can do bad all by myself. And don't even think about ever seeing little Nate again," Veronica unloaded. "I knew I shouldn't have given up the pussy the other night," she muttered to herself, further stinging him.

At the time, Mr. Smith thought his half-day delay in returning to Texas was worth the risk. After all, Detective Kane seemed convincing enough and there's no way his problem, the Black Ghost, would've seen it coming until it was too late. At least he thought so at the time. Besides, he hadn't been with a woman since being freed and the way Veronica made him feel when they were together was indescribable. Yes, he missed his wife, but this woman had a grip on his soul.

"Come. Now," Orlovsky's henchman tersely growled behind blank eyes after sliding open the van door. Mr. Smith wondered whether this one felt lucky or resentful for surviving the trap back in Texas. There was no room to park and they'd simply stopped in the middle of the street, tiny European cars behind them impatiently laying on their horns.

"Look...I gotta go," Piatkowski closed, no longer aroused as he was focused on staying alive. "We'll continue this conversation later."

"I'm serious, Nate. You might as well stay in Europe. Find some skinny bitch and start over because you ain't welcome here," she ended as she hung up.

The men led him inside same as always, except this time it was through the front door. People complained in French about them cutting the line, but were ignored. Another of those damned dance clubs, this one backlit in shades of blue and lavender catering to the youth and their need for an endless supply of bass drops, hallucinogens and amphetamines. In the past year, he'd lost track of how many in which they'd gathered for these meetings. It seemed Orlovsky had a plethora of these under his control and never met with anyone anywhere near where he laid his head.

The hulking man in black waited on him in the office off the dance floor where the music would mask any gunshots...or screams. The blonde Russian, while still impeccably dressed, forsook his traditional jacket or long sleeves for short sleeves and a vest tonight, displaying ornate tattoos on the pale arms he normally hid from regular folk. Here Mr. Smith was, former CIA, working with former Commie thugs; desperate bedfellows all with black hearts and bad intentions.

"So you come back here with your dick in your hand and the Black Ghost still alive?" Orlovsky immediately challenged him as soon as the door shut, isolating them from the sonic barrage. First it was Veronica, now the Russian with the put-downs and scolding. It wasn't like he hadn't assisted lining Orlovsky's pockets with more money than he ever could spend.

"We were very, very close," he replied with a fake smile, giving charm a try.

"Close was when I blew his bitch to hell in Paris and should've succeeded in killing him too if not for the police. You disappoint me. How do I know he didn't follow you here? To me? Huh?" Dimitri questioned as he pointed beyond the office window to the people gyrating and shaking on the dance floor.

"He didn't," he assured his irate, paranoid benefactor.

"And how are you so certain of this?" Dimitri followed up, looking his way again. Something about his tone made his men snap to attention; the non-verbal that goes on with people familiar with one another. The hot blonde who aided them in London with Al-Bin Sada sat in the corner, sipping on champagne and relishing whatever was to come.

"Because..." he tried to respond.

"Are you working with him now, *Piatkowski*?" Dimitri asked, almost mocking his name with a taunt-like sneer. "Is that how four of my best men don't return from America with you?"

"No! Of course not!" he replied, raising his voice with feigned concern. In reality, he couldn't care less about how many Orlovsky lost.

"Over the past week, I've lost way too many of my men, *Piatkowski*. Perhaps my methods here are brutal, so I trusted you when you said your ways would work in America, *Piatkowski*. And yet here you are with no results. Are you going to cost me more men with nothing to show for it, *Piatkowski*?" Dimitri accused more than he asked, his cold eyes squinting.

"Don't call me that. It's just 'Mr. Smith' now," he dared to correct him.

"Why? Are you ashamed of your Jew name, Jew? You think because of your Polish family's time in America, that you are somehow different?" Dimitri taunted as a vein bulged on the side of his neck. Smith had enough time in the field to be concerned. Even though his botched his leg years before in Afghanistan, he wasn't a total pushover when it came to fisticuffs.

"No. We're the same," he placated him. "And I can still be sure we both get what we want, friend."

"The same?" Dimitri questioned his audacity. "No, that's where you're wrong."

Dimitri had the numbers and Mr. Smith found both his arms pinned as the men snatched him off his feet and presented him to their boss like some sacrifice. He struggled, but soon found his face introduced to the office window's thick, tempered glass with a clunk from his skull. A swift punch to his kidneys halted his struggles. Mr. Smith groaned as he was firmly wedged against the glass, on display for the club-goers if they could see through the two-way mirror.

He heard the click of a safety being released followed by the touch of cool steel from a gun Orlovsky mashed against his skull.

"In fucking Paris, I was able to eliminate any trace of my involvement," the Russian began. "This? This is just a discotheque. You think those ants out there care if I blow your worthless American brains out? They just want to get high and have a good time. Hell, I just want to have a good time too once that black bastard is dead and gone. I need justice for my brothers and I need you to promise me that we'll do that together. Can you promise me, *Piatkowski*?"

"I told you. Call me 'Mr. Smith,'" he responded, figuring if he was dead he might as well go out with some dignity. At least his revenge on Al-bin Sada could give him solace in his final thoughts.

A lengthy pause gave him time to hear his heart beat over the music outside. Unable to move his head, his eyes searched for someone out there to look up and show some empathy before it all ended. Just one.

But no one did. It was a cold world after all.

Just when it seemed his heart would explode before his head, he fell to the floor. Dropped and dumped.

The office filled with Dimitri's roaring laughter which was joined by his men and the deadly blonde. "You've got balls, *Mr. Smith*. You'll live a while longer," he praised as he stowed his gun and poured himself a glass of vodka.

As Mr. Smith stood up and collected himself, he allowed a cold smile to form. A *while longer* was going to surpass his temporary business partner if he had anything to do with it.

ERIC PETE

25-Truth

Palermo, Sicily

I came close on my first try, but close don't count for shit. If we got to this third Orlovsky brother, we'd get to Piatkowski too. But from the little bit I'd learned from just his name surfacing in Paris, Dimitri wasn't as vulnerable or gullible as his deceased brothers. So here I was back in Europe taking a serious gamble to do it right once and for all.

At a place of their choosing, Joseline and I were meeting with a potential resource. As outlined in their explicit instructions, we drove to the overgrown outlines of an ancient fort then made a sharp left turn, driving four more kilometers until turning onto an unmarked road. Before long, we were met by rows of cars lining both sides of the winding road which ended at an old country estate.

"This is fucking insane," Joseline commented as she surveyed the assembled group of armed men and dogs who warily eyed our car.

"I know. But the element of surprise is gone now, so this is my way of making up for lost time. It'll be alright. Trust me," I tried assuring her with a smile as I unlocked the car doors, fully past the point of no return. Honestly, our fate was no longer our own as soon as we arrived on the island of Sicily.

After checking us for weapons, we were given the all clear and led to a courtyard around back. Five men, four of them elderly plus an unusually young one, sat around under the intense scrutiny of several armed men from different camps. They looked to their card game, barely paying us any mind as they drank their wine and engaged in small talk over scopa, an Italian card game.

"You have some nerve demanding this meeting and bringing only your woman," one of the older gentlemen griped in Italian.

"I assure you she's more than capable of handling herself should the need arise. But it definitely is not a demand," I humbly responded in kind using rough Italian in a heavy Ghanaian accent. I reached out of the Mafia families, posing as a representative of African interests, something not warmly received by these Italians on their home turf.

"Your boss is being disrespectful by not showing his face," he continued. "Respect is important."

"I understand. He would if he could, but there are some travel issues with getting into your country," I lied.

"Hmph," the one who looked to be only thirty or so scoffed while leering at Joseline. "It's not stopping the rest of your kind from flooding our country with your illegal immigrant filth."

I almost called him out on his racist, xenophobic bullshit with something about Sicily sharing a whole lotta history with Africa in the past, but bit my tongue. I wasn't here to pick a fight I was incapable of winning.

"Speak, African. What do you have to say, one-armed man?" a man with a full head of bushy black hair and a tiny mustache asked as he refilled his glass of vino.

"Dimitri Orlovsky," I began, suddenly garnering all their attention, even those who refused to glance our way. "We need the location and access to one of Orlovsky's men...with your blessing of course. We understand there one is within your territory that we are looking for."

"Why?" the younger one asked, anger in his eyes as he stood up from the card game. "This is none of our concern. Why should we help you?"

"Because you want to be rid of him yourselves, but are afraid," I boldly dared before clarifying my statement. "Afraid of disrupting your own business interests if you do so. And we understand that, but we all know that was no terrorist attack in Paris. As good as his connections, intimidation and payoffs have been, Orlovsky's crude methods will eventually have blowback. And how much longer before he takes those same tactics and uses them here in Italy? On you?"

"And why do you care about us? Were your employers the recipients of those methods?" another of the elders questioned, literally placing his cards on the table.

"Let's just say that people in Ghana have some import disputes with those Russians. All we're asking for is information on where to find this lieutenant in your territory. Your hands stay clean and we perhaps get a little dirty. Whether we win or lose, you no longer have to worry about Russian encroachment in your affairs for some time," I pitched with a grin, hoping I'd sold them enough bullshit.

"We don't deal with your kind," the first of the older Mafia heads popped off, still not sparing so much as a look our way as he rendered judgment. Joseline's foot slid in the soft dirt ever so slightly in reaction; she was about to take charge in her own way.

"Until you do. Which is now," I barked in defiance before my friend sprang into action.

"Kill them," he instructed, not bothering to even put it to a vote. "And don't leave a trace."

"You don't want to do this," I bluffed as the men surrounding us chambered their weapons, that familiar click-clack amplified by about twenty guns. The day had arrived when my words were no longer enough.

Joseline stepped forward, arms out as she revealed some kind marking in the webbing on her right hand, between the middle and index fingers. "You know what I am, Don Morici," she addressed the one who'd just ordered our deaths in perfect Italian. How'd she know his name?

"Just some dumb African bitch," the youngest Don cursed with a sneer. "Kill them."

"Wait. Come closer so I can see," Don Morici objected, suddenly motioning for the guards to let her approach their table. Was she trying to get within killing range of the Mafia heads or maybe just to snatch somebody's weapon to shoot our way out? Whatever the case, I was in the dark.

But Joseline did nothing other than let the old man examine her hand. He glanced up and nodded, removed his black wrap-around sunglasses, then nodded again.

"Let them go. And give them what they want. Let the fuckin' Russians pay the price," Don Morici ordered with a sigh as he massaged his brow.

∞

I didn't feel safe to speak until we were back on the Italian mainland, situated in a First Class cabin aboard the northbound Eurostar rail.

"What was that about back there on the island?" I asked Joseline, once the train attendant checked our boarding passes and moved on.

She held out her hand, fingers spread apart just as she did for that old man back in Sicily. What I assumed was just a scar between her knuckles from her line of work was actually a tiny brand. It was in the shape of an owl's head and looked ancient Greek or Mediterranean in its design.

"The owl is for the goddess Athena," she explained as if giving a history lecture. "The Nest has been around for a long time. The older folk in positions of power around the world know this and what we're capable of doing if crossed. Of course, Don Morici thinks I still belong to the Nest. That was enough to keep us from being ground up into spicy Italian sausage."

"I was gonna get us out of that without your help," I sulked, failing to convince even myself.

"No. Not this time," she commented, shaking her head. "Your play was desperate as it was, but at least you didn't play your accent like we were something outta *Coming to America*. If I'm going to protect you like I vowed, I need you to be honest. Are you gonna be able to hold up?"

"This...this is getting to me," I admitted, immediately regretting giving voice to it. Honesty made me feel like a failure in this moment, but I was broken down. Almost marching us into our own funeral is what really did it for me. "I feel like I'm off balance. And I don't mean just because of my arm. It's like I'm losing who I am in all this. I'm...I'm not really a killer."

"No shit. You're mad sloppy in the death game," she joked in her own sick way. "But effective when necessary from what I've seen. Even with your bum arm."

"I guess I've always kinda prided myself on being able to do worse with my tongue or misdirection."

"And you are a master, but we both know this is going to call for something more ruthless. More basic. More final," Joseline commented with a nod to herself as the train approached a tunnel.

"Yes. That's why I found you," I admitted as I grasped her hand. "I knew what was needed."

"Good. I like being needed," she said, almost flirtatiously. "But you need to be at your best. That pain you're keeping inside over your friend in Paris and whatever guilt you got over the married one back in Dallas? That shit gotta go somewhere. Let it go. Period. Because if I can't count on you, I can't protect you."

"You're right," I agreed, needing a reset back to my old self to see this through. Grieving and regret could come later when it was a luxury.

As I went about finding such a way back, Joseline intertwined her fingers with mine. She slowly rose then placed her other hand on my leg. I thought it was to steady herself in the moving car, but her balance was impeccable, nothing an accident. She squeezed my knee then looked me in my eyes. I politely smiled, my pulse racing a little bit as she slid her hand up my thigh. She was simple, direct...and quick. With my other arm stuck in its sling, she found no resistance as she unzipped my pants and fished around my boxers. Hell, my dick hardened so fast, it almost popped her in the face. She smiled while taking me in her hand.

"Nice. You got a permit for this?" she complimented as she stroked me, uncaring if somebody happened into our car.

"What are you doing?" I asked, questioning her timing, but not the effect of her efforts.

"Isn't it obvious? You're a man. I'm helping you get your head in the game," she coyly replied as my breathing turned ragged at her touch.

My dick danced, its head eagerly throbbing as she bent down and dragged her tongue lazily over the tip. Reluctance and resistance were banished from my thoughts with each kiss she sloppily bestowed upon my royal scepter. Between my moans and groans, she removed her designer thong and draped it across my face. I breathed deeply of the intoxicating mix of perfume and her honeyed treasure, closing my eyes as I gave in to something primal that tickled the back of my brain since our first encounter in Boston.

While writhing in my seat and wanting more of her creative intervention, Joseline hiked her skirt up her thighs and mounted me. As the train entered the tunnel, plunging us into darkness, I entered her and plunged into her darkness.

"Give it to me. Give me all that pain," she urged in my ear as she ground down on me, welcoming me with a hot, sticky greeting. She bucked as I rose up, throwing my hips in deep, measured thrusts. She coaxed me with those powerful thighs of hers, imploring me to quicken my pace. "Don't quit on me, boy," she demanded in a demeaning yet *hot as fuck* way.

During the brief flashes of light as the train raced along, I watched her head arch back, wildly throwing her body around as if gripped by insanity. Yeah, it was crazy to be doing this here and now, but fuck it. I followed her, startled yet pleased with how wonderful madness like this could be.

I wasn't quitting on her and I certainly wasn't quitting until my enemies' heads were displayed on my wall.

Maybe Joseline was right about this getting my head in the game.

ERIC PETE

26-Truth

Genoa, Italy

"You're staring at me again," she admonished as I did just what she was accusing me of.

"Can't help it. You're all I can see," I acknowledged from my vantage point slightly below deck as the boat bobbed along. "But it's not like I'm complaining," I mumbled to myself. The red bikini on her glistening brown skin was banging.

"Well, at least make yourself useful. Throw me the sunscreen," Joseline requested as she repositioned her booty atop the deck. I complied and tossed it underhanded, which she snatched from the air without even looking. While she squeezed the tube into her hands and rubbed the protection onto her arms and shoulders, I wiped the sweat from my brow and listened for any approaching craft. With scant cloud cover, it was uncomfortable being fully clothed without a breeze and my arm sling made it more nerve wracking.

"What's taking him so long?" I complained as I raised my head topside and peered out. The cigar boat strafed the waters all afternoon, zigzagging on the Mediterranean like it was his own personal playground yet still hadn't taken the bikini-clad bait.

"Patience, oh ye of little faith," Joseline timely remarked, adjusting her sunglasses as she stood up. She wasn't just stretching. This was the sign that we were a go. She yanked on the rigging, sending a sail tumbling onto the deck.

With a wink my way, she took a few steps then dropped into the water with a scream uncharacteristic of her nature. I heard the cigar boat gun its motor amid the frantic sounds of a damsel in distress. It eased back on the throttle as it came alongside us and the sail boat dipped on the waves beneath the weight of two men coming aboard.

They cleared and secured the loose sail then offered a hand to the treading Joseline. After they helped her back aboard, the important one joined them; possessing a gritty face and jet black hair, yet looking every bit the newly minted Euro-douche in linen clothes and designer loafers.

"I'm sorry. I was admiring your boat and got careless as I dropped sail," Joseline giggled before coughing up the little bit of seawater she swallowed.

"Why is a pretty girl like you sailing alone? No husband?" the scarred thug Sergei Malenkov quizzed in his rough English.

"Nope. Just little ole me," she replied, batting her eyelashes.

"Don't let the breathtaking surroundings fool you. It can be quite dangerous around here. Perhaps, my men and I can accompany you. We have caviar and plenty of champagne on my boat," he offered just as he motioned for his men to check below deck. Not even Joseline's beauty and charms could dull his suspicious nature. And that nature was easy to predict.

I took a step into the open, shooting the closest one in the head while I still had the element of surprise. The second one was fast though and already aiming at me, sure to find his mark. That is, until Joseline delivered a timely spinning heel kick to the back of his head. He stumbled past me and fell, awkwardly landing face first at the bottom of the stairs, his neck bent at an unnatural angle.

That left Malenkov situated between me; one-armed, but armed; and an equally dangerous Joseline.

"Hmm. So no caviar or champagne for us then," he sighed as he surrendered, putting his hands in the air. "But I must warn you; if you're trying to rob rich people, you've made a serious mistake. Do you know who I am?" he bragged. Yeah. We did. Malenkov was just another opportunistic thug muscling in on the Port of Genoa's cargo and shipping action for the Russians. Something the Mafia dons hadn't yet nipped in the bud until now, but he served a much more valuable purpose to me.

"Yeah. I think we do know who you are," I smartly replied as I handed off my gun to Joseline. I nudged the bloodied, still body of his other guard with my foot. Certain of my work, I kicked him down the stairs atop his friend then grabbed a gas can, dousing both and splashing the stairs and deck as well. "You're our transportation out of here," I said as I dropped a lit cigarette lighter below deck.

27-Joseline

So as not to insult him, we roughed up Sergei Malenkov upon reaching the shore; otherwise, he wouldn't have taken us seriously. And that was after killing his two men on the boat. Just a swollen face, chipped teeth and some bruised ribs, but it got his attention. Afterwards, we left him tied to a chair in an empty basement apartment, cursing in Russian for hours while loud Italian wedding songs blared into his ears. Figuring he'd stewed enough, we returned to the building under renovation to check on our progress.

"You'll regret this," Orlovsky's man threatened Truth as I snatched the headphones from his ringing ears. "My men will skin you alive when they find me. But first we'll rape your bitch and make you watch. Maybe rape you too."

When Truth came over to speak, Malenkov spat in his face. Truth didn't let it faze him, but I backhanded the Russian twice just because I felt like it. The fucker, even with his swollen eye, seemed to like it rough, laughing as he winked at me.

"We have our hands on you, Sergei. Just by this, you should be dead. Either you're very lucky and have some value to us...or you're worthless and...," Truth said with a shrug, allowing our captive to piece it together as he circled around and around, always on the periphery of the Russian's vision. I think that unnerved our guest more than the threats.

"What is it you want? How much is it going to cost for me to be back in some presentable clothes?" the criminal asked, still playing tough.

"We don't want your money, you smug bastard," Truth explained. In his outburst, he stumbled slightly then regained his balance, his own pain and exhaustion showing. He probably yearned for another of those pain pills he'd been discretely chewing like candy.

"Then what? Spell it out for me and let us be done with these games," Malenkov begged.

"We don't want the lapdog. We want the top dog," Truth replied, complying. "Give us Orlovsky."

"If you know what I am then you know I would never do that," he vowed, reminding us he was a Vor through and through.

Outside the front door, I noticed a shadow pass beneath it. It could've been a stray dog or some random person, but I didn't deal in glass half-full kinds of shit.

"I need some air. I'll be right back," I told Truth, deciding to check it out alone and leave him to getting his answers.

"We'll be here," Truth said calmly with a smile as he surveyed the tools I'd laid out to make the Russian more compliant.

Closing the door behind me, I dashed to the back of the complex and up a narrow alleyway. I didn't find dog nor cat; just eerie silence as I slowly drew a blade from my belt. I looked around, appearing lost or confused on the cobblestones while waiting to draw in whoever it was.

"Metu," the woman who thought she snuck up behind me challenged.

"Nomini," I answered the challenge in a language used only by us. In relief, I turned to face Amanda, the name I always used because I never could pronounce her real Afghan name. I stowed my blade and we embraced as sisters.

"We heard somebody invoked our name in Sicily. From the description, I figured it was you, Sister," Amanda said, her tan skin and almond eyes still otherworldly to behold. In her white blouse and khaki shorts, she was pretty unassuming.

"What do you want?" I asked my fellow killer.

"For you to return to the Nest," she replied. "You've been hard to find. We're not going to lose track of you this time."

"That's never going to happen. I enjoy my freedom way too much. It was time for me to go," I let her know.

"Why are you back in Europe then?" she pondered.

"A vow I made to someone. I'm keeping my promise and seeing it through to the end."

"A promise. To that broken American back there?" she asked, letting me know she'd been following us for longer than she let on. Like some silly teenager, I nervously wondered if she spied us on the train. Amanda always excelled at tracking and concealment. "You broke your vow to us when you left, so why is this different?"

"That 'broken American'? He needs me. You? The Nest will continue to do just fine without me," I blew off.

"Shall I tell the rest what you said?"

"Don't matter, Sister. If you or any of the Nest have an issue with me, I'll deal with it at that time."

"Maybe I should just kill your friend. If he's gone, so is your vow," Amanda rationalized in a way I couldn't tell was threat or joke.

"You're welcome to try. But you know how that would end," I urged somewhat forcefully as I sized up her way too few weaknesses and how to use my surroundings to my advantage.

"Relax. I'm just messing with you, Joseline," Amanda laughed as she playfully squeezed my shoulder, rubbing deeply with her thumb. Over our years together growing up in service to the Nest, our bonds of sisterhood extended beyond mere comradery and that part of me responded to her touch. "What's your mission, Sister?" she asked.

"Dimitri Orlovsky. We were loosening up one of his lieutenants when you tried to be sneaky back there," I replied.

"I allowed you to spot me. It's been too long since we've spoken...or since I've seen your face," she admitted, our eyes meeting. "Guess I'll let you get back to it then. Be well and 'til next time, Sister. Nomini."

"Metu," I replied this time hoping this was our final encounter. If the Nest were to ask her directly, she'd have to tell them she saw me. And if I saw Amanda under those terms, it wouldn't be nothin' nice.

"Oh," she added as if an afterthought when it really wasn't. "One of our sisters is working for Orlovsky. So I guess you're really not done with the Nest after all."

Troubled by Amanda's parting shot, I returned to the apartment, ready to continue our session. Truth sat in a backwards-turned chair directly in front of Malenkov. All the tools on the table were untouched and Malenkov was still alive, untouched as well. A yellow puddle on the floor pooled around his feet and he sobbed, trying to keep it in check, but his painful gulps and hard swallows the telling sign.

"...What did I miss?" I asked in surprise. I hadn't been gone that long and I was very puzzled by the scene.

"Nothing. Me and my friend Sergei just had a talk," Truth answered in a dark, smug kind of way, his chest heaving with pride. Truth had regained himself in breaking this man; a surgeon regaining the use of his hands...so to speak. "We're done now."

"You...you're not going to let me live, are you?" the man asked rhetorically as his whimpering subsided and semblance of pride returned.

"If the piss covered Gucci loafers were on the other foot...," Truth answered with a sigh as he looked into the man's eyes. He nodded as I grabbed the gun from the table, placed the silencer tip to Malenkov's head and squeezed the trigger once.

28

Lyon, France

Mr. Smith had fallen out of favor, no longer enjoying the freedom he'd taken for granted. Indeed, he had traded a hopeless dungeon for a gilded cage. He no longer hung from his wrists to be poked and prodded by a sadistic Sheikh, but now an uncertain fate was more unnerving. Since returning from the States, he was constantly under someone's watchful eye, uselessly sitting on his ass in either a club or tiny apartment, waiting on Orlovsky to decide what to do with him. Some days, Orlovsky treated him as nearly an equal. Other times, there was no hiding the disdain the Russian had for him. As much as he'd helped him raid the Sheikh's assets, this was unfair. They'd even begun monitoring his calls to Veronica in New Orleans, mocking in Russian their arguments and his groveling. No respect, but it was not unexpected. He was just a resource and nothing more.

Orlovsky took it personal, the loss of so many of his best men between the streets of Paris and on Smith's failed mission in America. He'd refilled the ranks of his dark enterprise with fresh bodies from Russia and Eastern Europe, but they were neither as loyal nor as ruthless as he was accustomed. There was blame to go around for the failings, but Mr. Smith was a most convenient scapegoat.

Tonight, Mr. Smith was to stay around one of Orlovsky's more successful French clubs like some sort of dutiful mistress, barely seen and rarely heard. On the other side of the two-way mirror, celebrities and wannabes humped, danced and mingled to near capacity. This was a big night and the whole place pulsated from the sounds of the top rate DJ with which Orlovsky had replaced his regular man. He and his men feasted on the steady supply of vodka, coke and women in celebration, slurring their English words so badly that Mr. Smith was left to piece together what was said on his own.

After a sharp knock, one of Orlovsky's henchmen entered. From his attire, he wasn't part of tonight's festivities and looked to be shivering.

"What's the matter, boy? Your devushka kicked you out?" one of the men teased about his girlfriend.

"They...they hit our distribution on the Rhone. Our shipment...The entire warehouse is in flames," the young man in the leather jacket reluctantly replied. Orlovsky used the main river for import and distribution of his narcotics in and out of France from the Mediterranean.

Those in the office who heard him were immediately stunned from their collective high. The rest soon joined in, quickly realizing something in the room had changed.

"Who is 'they'? It's just one man. One!" the large man screamed as he cast a hateful gaze Mr. Smith's way. "Everybody, get out! Now!" Orlovsky yelled, meaning the women and any civilians.

"How are you so certain it's him?" Mr. Smith posed to his not-so-benevolent benefactor. "I'm sure you have other enemies."

"And you are a fool now, Smith? My man Sergei's missing in Genoa. That's how the Black Ghost found out about my distribution hub. He must know I'm helping you, Mr. Smith. So he's trying to hurt me by going after my money," Orlovsky surmised, sounding paranoid and way too drunk.

Despite wishing Orlovsky was merely deluded, Mr. Smith knew how resourceful the black stranger whose true name he never learned could be. If he did track him down here to France so quickly, it wouldn't be much longer...one way or another.

"What do you want me to do?" Mr. Smith asked, looking for any excuse to get away from this fuckin' club with its horrible music and put some distance between the two of them.

"You? Nothing. You are worthless. Just watch and see how it's done," Orlovsky replied to Smith. "Have all the contacts around town looking for this bastard. Pay them double. Triple if they bring me his head," he instructed his key people.

"We don't need to," one of too many men named Sasha stated with a cell phone to his ear. "It's our friend with Interpol. The black was spotted checking into a hotel in Corbas yesterday. The Cris Hotel."

"See! I told you it was him! The Black Ghost!" Orlovsky taunted Smith, his red eyes ablaze with the fire of vindication. He then turned his attention to his men. "We'll worry about the warehouse and our losses tomorrow. Tell our friend to keep the authorities back and send everyone to Corbas. Don't let him slither out a window or any crack. If he's not there when you arrive, wait for him."

"You're not going?" Mr. Smith asked in surprise.

"No," Orlovsky replied, gritting his teeth and taking Smith's question as an affront. "There's too much going on tonight. I have to be here...for appearances."

"I know this man. He's the most devious person I've ever gone up against. He's probably herding your men into a trap," Mr. Smith offered. He'd toyed with keeping his mouth shut; that is, until Orlovsky revealed he wasn't going.

"Dah," Orlovsky agreed with a smile as he downed a shot of vodka. "This is why you are going with them; his little trap be damned. Because you'll kill him this time...or my men will kill you. Ponyat?"

"Yes. I understand," Smith grimaced.

ERIC PETE

29-Truth

Lyon, France

"*Attack him where he is unprepared, appear where you are not expected.*" -Sun Tzu, The Art of War

"*I came in the door. I said it before.*"-Rakim, Eric B. Is President

"Bonjour, Monsieur Spielberg," the bearded man in black greeted me as he reviewed the guest list, his head lowered and too absorbed with striking another name. When I cleared my throat, he looked up and finally noticed the size of our group, a staged entourage and security detail made up of paid extras courtesy of the local theatre troupe. "Um...well, we have you and your guest on the list," he continued, referring to Joseline only.

"My guest?" I loudly scoffed while laughing on the inside. "You've never heard of Harmonica? She's only the biggest trending sensation in all of Finland." Joseline didn't know what I was going to say until then; but with her pink wig, black feather boa, leopard print dress and thigh high boots; the cheesier and more pretentious my act, the better.

"Well...I," the man too old for his man-bun stuttered to say.

"And you better have our entire party on that list, little man. The internet has been buzzing about this place and we plan on spending plenty Euros in this bitch tonight. With my girl's Instagram followers, you're gonna be begging her to come back," I verbally bombarded him. All this commotion helped distract from my useless arm, so I didn't mind pretending I was above shaking hands.

"My apologies, Monsieur. Of course you and your entire party are welcome," he relented as I knew he would. "It's just been a very hectic night to say the least and we are adjusting to the volume as best we can. Allow me to have you and your party seated in VIP immediately with a dozen bottles of our best French champagne, compliments of the house."

"Well...that'll do for now, but this night better not disappoint. Trust me, you're gonna want Harmonica's hashtag to be a 'good' hashtag," I persisted.

"Oh. And Monsieur?" Joseline followed my lead for the finishing touch. "Get you some better fitting clothes and a haircut if you plan on keeping your job. This place is supposed to impress, no?"

Glad to be through with us, security opened the oversized double doors after the barest of pat-downs for weapons. And just like that, we came right in the front door, entering the snake pit with style and flair.

"I look stupid, by the way," Joseline murmured in my ear as she pretended to kiss me before curious and admiring eyes.

"Girl, that's all Balmain you're rockin'. So act right," I corrected her with a haughty laugh before the club's sound system drowned me out.

I hadn't used my Elvis Spielberg persona, an over-the-top filthy rich identity fitting an event such as this, in years. Knowing this was Orlovsky's most recent hangout, I had the club leaked as the new "it" spot for those wanting to be seen in Lyon. Rumors from Kanye & the Kardashians to a One Direction reunion to the Weeknd to Taylor Swift dropping in tonight were spread all over Twitter and my little friend's 4Shizzle gossip site, which had Orlovsky's guest list bursting at the seams. To keep it going, I tossed some Euros around to random people who relayed fake celebrity sightings around Lyon on social media.

Orlovsky had his crime and war game on lock, but like most powerful men, he was restless and, deep down, in need of acceptance. That's what moved him from the back alleys of Moscow and Kiev into the streets of Europe. He wanted to move up in the world and trade the shadows for the light. Tonight, I was giving him a big, glowing ball of acceptance in which to bask. But with light there usually comes heat.

And it was gonna get a whole lot hotter before the night was over.

In the VIP, Joseline and I pretended to take selfies, but my phone was actually a scanner.

"There's the office," I said to Joseline as my phone detected the warm bodies behind the two-way mirror below the DJ's booth. "And it is crowded."

"Orlovsky? That asshole spook Piatkowski?"

"Probably. Looks like they're celebrating...for now," I remarked as I tried to improve the resolution. But it was too far away with too many people dancing between them and us.

"Oh my gawd. Did Leonardo DiCaprio just wave at me?" Joseline giggled as she lowered her sunglasses.

"You look fuckin' hot. Probably wants to add you to his supermodel entourage," I replied without a glance, amused my campaign attracted some real celebrities tonight.

"Truth, why were you so sure this approach would work?" she asked with a toss of her boa before sipping some more of the Moët & Chandon. I told her to enjoy herself and she certainly was.

"Trust me. I have a lot of experience in the entertainment industry and settings like this. My...uncle was once the head of On-Phire Records," I volunteered, remembering the day I ended his life not too far away from here, in Monaco.

"Holy shit! Your uncle was Jason North?" Joseline gasped over the pounding bass drop as the crowd went wild and confetti fell from the ceiling.

"You know about rap music and hip-hop?" I asked in surprise. Kinda expected she was too busy at her finishing school getting all prim and proper.

"Duh. Of course. Even if I didn't, anyone with even the most basic knowledge of pop culture knows who Jason North was. Let's see," she said as she summoned a thought. "He had that rapper AK...Oh! And that boyband Saint Roch...before Jonas Barfield blew up on his own. You were part of all that?"

"More like 'behind the scenes'," I replied, keeping some of my darker duties to myself even amongst a kindred spirit such as she. "Come dance with me, Harmonica," I said with a grin, needing to get closer to that office, but also to change the subject.

I checked my watch as we wormed our way to the center of the main dance floor. This morning, we'd rigged Orlovsky's warehouse on the river with enough explosives to blow it sky high. By my reckoning, it went boom about thirty minutes ago. By the speed with which one of Orlovsky's men rushed into his office, he was about to get some very bad news.

Within minutes, prostitutes streamed from the office like someone had farted in a phone booth. Pleased, I spun Joseline around with my good arm then pulled her close.

"Truth?" she called out, her wig a little crooked, but still too sexy to look very foolish.

"Yeah?" I responded.

"If you could be somewhere else right now," she began, an odd tone to her voice. Maybe it was the champagne. "If none of this was necessary and if the two of us happened to be somewhere else...together, where would you pick?"

I thought deeply about her scenario, the music briefly disappearing as I tuned it out. Instead, I focused on Joseline, someone as much a shadow as me. Perhaps, in some imaginary world of our making, there could be substance formed from our shared void. I conjured up rocky shores and wave crashing along a beach. Behind us were our footprints in the sand. No more death. No more chaos. "Wait. What's going on?" I asked, shaking it off and dispelling such fanciful dreams.

"We don't have to go forward with this. We can leave now. These odds...aren't good," she said with a shake of her head. "And with only you and three good arms between the both of us, I can't be sure we come out of this in one piece."

"What aren't you telling me?" I probed, unnerved by what I perceived to be diminished resolve in her. What could have her shaken?

"Orlovsky has someone working for him," she answered as she failed to look me in my eye.

"Yeah, a whole lot of someones," I chuckled as I put my hand under her chin and gently raised her head. "But with what I got out of our friend back in Genoa, they're all accounted for."

"No. You're not hearing me," she said harshly. "Someone like me, Truth. But maybe better."

"Here?" I paused, taken aback by this news.

"I don't know. Could be anywhere his interests lie," she stated, tentatively monitoring anyone dancing close by. "But if he suspects someone like me is helping you, then it would be wise to keep her handy."

I nodded my head as the music suddenly felt louder, the confines tighter.

"Go," I calmly said in her ear, recalculating it all. Joseline was a jewel and I wasn't worth risking her life on. Sophia and those innocents in Paris were enough.

"Huh?"

"Go," I urged a little more strongly. "You've got me this far and I appreciate it. But I ain't runnin' no matter what I face. They die tonight," I professed.

"What? You can't do this alone. Are you fuckin' crazy?" Joseline barked as she shoved me. The revelers laughed at the perceived lovers' quarrel.

"I've been crazy since I came out my momma. But I got this," I stated as I sent a text. And someone across the Atlantic received it, waiting until now to send a false report disguised as an Interpol alert on someone fitting my description.

I got this, I tried convincing myself as I cast my gaze toward the office and waited.

30-Truth

"Go on. Get out of here," I ordered Joseline again.

"No. This doesn't work without me," she was sure to remind.

"Then you seriously underestimate me. And overestimate your worth," I tried convincing her.

"Fuck you. I'm not leaving," she urged with a laugh at my attempt at getting under her skin.

I held my phone up again pretending to engage in selfie time. Behind the two-way mirror, the tallest man in the room, who I presumed to be Orlovsky, waved his arms. I tried to figure out which one might be Mr. Smith, but without eyeballing him, it would be pure guesswork. Before anyone got suspicious, I put my phone down and kept dancing with Joseline as she backed her ass against me and reached up, wrapping her arms around my neck. More confetti fell as people began singing along with the DJ's latest hit, the night steady building higher and higher. Under the cover of the smoke machines and excessive blaring horns, a bunch of men cleared out from the office, filled with bad intentions. A hotel in the nearby town of Corbas was about to get way too much attention.

"You sure about staying, *Harmonica*?" I asked her, back to smiling as I relented.

"Wouldn't miss it for the world, *Elvis*," Joseline replied as she dropped her boa on the crowded floor. In her hands, two ceramic blades mysteriously appeared between strobe flashes. I popped my lapel collar, coming out with a single undetectable blade of my own.

I held my phone up a final time and looked through the camera scanner.

"Less than five bodies inside," I called out to Joseline as I pretended to snap a picture of the DJ as he stood atop his turntables and whipped the crowd into a frenzy.

"Manageable," she said like all cold and tactical-like. "How many you count in our way?"

"Three. Unless there are some stragglers in the hallway," I said while pretending to tell her a joke.

"I count three as well," she remarked with a nod then a fake laugh.

We moved in the direction of Orlovsky's office as indirectly as possible, going with the ebb and flow of the crowd in what appeared to be a random pattern to any onlooker. As we approached our first obstacle in the private area off the main stage labeled "Employees Only", a few additional men exited the office.

"It's him," I gasped, stopping in my tracks as I recognized Piatkowski in the group. His mind was elsewhere and he didn't even look my way. Shit. Not only were both my targets in the same place, I now was in danger of losing one.

"I know, Truth. I see him too. Don't lose it now," Joseline said as she placed a calming hand on my shoulder, the blade still concealed by her fingers. "First things first; we get to the office. We don't want a shootout in here with all these civilians."

"I can't let him get away," I complained, wanting to ignore the plan and make a run at him.

"If he's going to the hotel in Corbas, we can get him later," she reminded me. "Orlovsky's the real danger; the one with the will and the resources. So get your head in the game before I decide to gut you on the spot."

She was right. It was Orlovsky's smug face who, on his orders, blew up Sophia after stalking us like dogs on the Paris streets.

"Alright. Let's go. First one up," I pressed on as we engaged our plan to succeed with minimal violence for a change.

Joseline took the lead, assaulting the Russian with a request to take a selfie while I strolled by. She nicked him with a finger nail, showing faux concern as he suddenly became ill, his stomach convulsing from the fast acting poison. I walked up on the second line of defense, asking for him to use the restroom.

"Move back. Restrooms over there," he replied in his bad English, not interested in small talk, but willing to show his sidearm.

"Hey, big sexy man!" Joseline gushed as she sashayed up to the man. He was about to growl at her until she stuck her tongue down his throat. I was taken by surprise, but not as much as the man who suddenly experienced her ceramic blade repeatedly piercing between his ribs. He grabbed at her which she pretended was an attempt to paw her ass. As the light faded from his eyes, internal wounds in abundance, she leaned him onto a nearby chair and placed her sunglasses on him. After borrowing his gun, she snagged a half empty bottle of champagne off the table and nodded at me. Ready, we continued our steady march to the real target.

"Can I help you?" the last guardian directly outside the office door asked upon seeing us. We kept walking in his direction, laughing as if engrossed in our own conversation with no idea we were in a restricted area.

"Don't worry about me with Orlovsky. Once we get past this one, I need you to go after Mr. Smith," I whispered in her ear as the man called out to us again, not sensing a threat from brightly dressed drunk rich folk.

"*Who*?" she asked, confused.

"Piatkowski," I clarified while shaking my head.

"Oh, that's right. Gotcha. Y'all spy types got more fuckin' aliases than rappers," she joked.

She charged forward, playing drunk as she held her acquired bottle at her side.

"You there!" she hissed at the guard. "I will not tolerate such shitty service. Is this the best champagne you have? I know you keep the best stuff in your office!"

He shoved her back into my arms and was about to pull his gun out.

"I'm sorry, mate. She's a wee bit tipsy," I apologized for her as she kept slurring her words and cursing about champagne.

"Both of you need to go back," he told me, figuring I was the reasonable one. Joseline staggered off to the side as I engaged him.

"And that's exactly what I was telling her. But you know how women are when they get their minds made up," I rattled off.

"What's wrong with your arm?" he asked, being the first one in the club to notice it. His eyes flared with recognition, but that was at the same time Joseline clocked him with the champagne bottle.

Then she did it again.

And again.

Each blow in time to the beat of the music.

It was a solid bottle indeed with blunt force being less noisy than gunshots going off and alerting Orlovsky behind the door. When she finished, half the man's face was caving in, his body twitching as blood bubbled up through what used to be his nose and mouth.

"Whew," she exclaimed, wiping the tiny red splatters from her face as her chest heaved. Her grin was unsettling and reminded me that bloodlust sometimes dwells in even the most attractive of packages. She tossed his weapon to me, seeing as he'd never use it again nor any higher brain functions.

"Thank you," I said to her as I chambered a round in the Stoeger nine millimeter. I had some difficulty due to the hand I kept to my side, but tried to pretend it was nothing.

"Still want me to get after Mr. Smith?" she queried, deep concern etched on her brow.

"Yes," I answered resolutely.

"No matter what's on the other side of that door?" she followed up in a skeptical manner.

"Yes. Now hurry. You'll have the element of surprise coming up behind him," I urged. "After that...you're free from your debt."

She didn't bother trying to talk me out of it any longer. With a shrug and her eyes bidding me goodbye, she sped off in her thigh high boots. If she killed Piatkowski, even better, but that wasn't my real motive for making her go after him. Truth be told, Joseline had better survival odds out there on the streets than in this tight confined club; even if it left me at a disadvantage.

Turning to face the office door, I tried to remember everyone's position inside from my earlier scan. One good hand, a ceramic blade and a full clip were all I had.

But it was gonna work. With duct tape and determination, I'd make it work. And after he joined his two brothers, the Orlovsky line would be over.

I took a single step back and delivered a side kick to the door, splintering it where the knob meets the frame. As it swung open, I grinned; more from nerves than actual joy.

"*This is for you, Sophia. I guess you finally got me killed,*" I mumbled to myself as I squeezed the trigger, firing away as I ran inside to what was a certain death.

ERIC PETE

31-Truth

There were six of them in the office when I barged in, gun a blazin'; five men and a coked out blonde who must've missed the memo to leave before the fun began. Without taking my eyes off my true target, I shot one of the men dead in the chest as he sprang from the couch.

Orlovsky was the tallest man in the room; the same grinning figure who gave the order to fire that grenade launcher back in Paris. He wasn't grinning this time nor did he look as confident minus the element of surprise. As big as he was, he was deceptively quick, dodging my bullet like he'd been shot at all his life. I didn't get the luxury of another crack at him, using another of my sparse rounds to shoot one of his crew before he could do likewise.

Struck in his throat, the man's automatic rifle flailed around with his finger still on the trigger, letting loose a barrage of bullets that peppered the room. Everyone ducked for cover, but one of the men wasn't quite fast enough and paid the price. With a round ripping through his torso and another drilled into his thigh, he crumbled to his knees, screaming like a maniac.

"Dimitri Orlovsky!" I called out from behind the overturned sofa that doubled as shelter. "Do you always surround yourself with such dumb-asses? Your man in Genoa was eager to give you up. I couldn't get him to stop talking," I taunted while checking my clip.

"You!" Orlovsky roared as he rose to his feet, towering and menacing once again. Unarmed and uncaring, he rumbled toward me, cracking his knuckles along the way. But he wasn't unarmed for long. He took the wailing, wounded man's gun from his hand then, with no hesitation, used the man's own 45 caliber pistol to silence him permanently. Dimitri was cold as fuck and with no conscience.

He fired repeatedly in my direction, yelling to draw me out while spouting some gibberish in Russian about a "Black Ghost". The couch wasn't the best shield; the stuffing afloat around my face foreshadowing it was only a matter of time before I had an unwanted hole in me too.

I popped up and returned fire, spotting his last remaining man creeping up from the side, more methodical than his boss, but with an Israeli assault rifle held close and ready. If I didn't get my hand on one of the loose weapons on the floor with a little more bang, I hadn't a chance. I took a deep breath before squirting out the other end of the overturned couch, shooting random cover fire behind me as I scrambled. Orlovsky and his last man scattered, but still shot back at me, barely missing. Like some slick action hero, I slid to a stop in the middle of the floor, dropping my handgun while simultaneously kicking the unused assault rifle from the man I'd shot in the throat up in the air.

I caught it and squeezed the trigger, knowing I had better hit somebody, but only succeeded in shattering the two way mirror, exposing us for everyone to see. Orlovsky let out a defiant laugh as the booming music that had, til now, masked the sounds of warfare; washed over the office in a tidal wave of sound. Behind him, the panicked clubgoers took off scurrying for their lives. Still, that rash display by him made for a sure target and I wasn't going to let it slip by again. I squeezed the trigger, prematurely pleased with my accomplishment.

Instead of Orlovsky engulfed in a bloody hail of bullets, I was greeted by an impotent clicking sound.

"Fuck!" I cursed over the gun jam, my hand trembling in frustration. I was too close, but with only one good arm, I'd never clear the weapon in time. Orlovsky's man saw my predicament and took advantage, unloading a full clip at me. I leapt to avoid the assault rifle's spray, but as it violently peppered the floor, a round grazed my ankle. I yelped in pain, barely limping the final meter before rolling across Orlovsky's large desk. More shots followed, Orlovsky joining in the open hunt as I tumbled onto my head, my neck sending searing daggers of pain through my body that mixed with those from my already damaged arm and now bleeding ankle.

On the floor behind the desk, I took a millisecond to succumb to the fatigue, before straining to right myself. Opening my eyes to assess my dire predicament, I found I had company.

"Mon dieu, mon dieu," the blonde hooker in the fetal position beside me recited over and over, probably going into shock. Shit.

While I tried to figure out what to do with her, Orlovsky's voice grew louder; his throaty taunts booming now instead of the DJ's programmed music that had ceased. Maybe the police would rush in and save the day, but I doubted it. Especially with a warehouse explosion and fire on the river to divert their attention. And the longer I stayed pinned down, the greater chance some of his backup would arrive.

"You try to come at me by yourself? Me?" my tormentor boasted. "Who the fuck do you think you are, little man?"

I pinned the unreliable assault rifle between my feet and frantically worked to clear the jammed round from the chamber. But I was too nervous, so of course it didn't cooperate. Just out of sight, Orlovsky and his man were still there, steady pressing their advantage.

After a rare moment of unnerving silence, one of them hurled a Molotov cocktail at the very desk behind which the two of us sought shelter. The vodka bottle exploded in a ball of glass shards, depositing its flaming contents all over and giving me flashbacks of my arm afire in Paris. The blonde girl screamed in a panic, but I kept as quiet I could, trying to come up with a plan. Every extra minute I stayed alive was a victory.

"Do I smell something burning?" he taunted, seemingly not caring for the woman pinned down with me or whether his club went up in flames. "You haunted and tormented my brother Vasili until he took his own life! Tonight, I will roast you in his memory, my little chorn!"

"Fuck you!" I replied in his native tongue as smoke began to fill the office.

Tendrils of blue flame rolled down the sides of the desk right where my face was pressed. I pulled away reflexively and barely missed getting my head blown off. The flames danced amidst the splintering wood as his man with the assault rifle sprayed the desk with several more probing rounds, meant to make me move.

"Votre nom?" I asked the blonde, still balled up and rocking to and fro.

"Aimée," she replied in barely a murmur as Orlovsky's growl, mere feet from us, grew more menacing.

"Aimée, when I stand up and start shooting back, I need you to go. Just crawl out of here toward that side door and don't look back," I instructed in French, hoping I hadn't botched the translation in my haste.

"No! No! They'll shoot me! I'm scared!" she frantically replied, finally peeling a hand back to reveal part of her face, dark mascara streaks beneath a glazed eye.

I guess that was good as I had nothing to shoot and really didn't want to make myself a target anyway. But that left me with the unenviable alternative to stay cowering behind a burning desk like some coward and wait for the inevitable.

Footsteps crunched atop broken glass and drywall fragments as the shots crept closer and closer, unnerving in their pauses. I leaned into the desk, to see if it would move under my weight, but it was too solid and heavy. Time to come out and do my best to take at least one of them with me. I began tugging on desk drawers, figuring to use one as a club or something.

Battered muscles and a bloody, sore ankle tensed for what was to come as I counted mere nanoseconds between shots and them hitting their target.

"You never should have come to Europe, you arrogant bastard. You should've kept running like the little black mouse you are," Orlovsky boasted in between bullet spray. Like wild jackals, they knew they had me and took pleasure in fucking with their prey. The woman placed her hand on my shoulder and I reached back, patting it in vain to try to comfort her. The innocents in Paris were in the wrong place at the wrong time as well.

I was naïve in thinking I had more time though. A large thud atop the flaming desk gained my attention. I looked up to see Orlovsky's remaining soldier leering at me, his muzzle squarely pointed at my head.

"Boss says you're a ghost. You're no ghost. Ghosts don't bleed. And they don't die," he taunted in Russian with a wink.

A shrill whistle from outside the office walls distracted him before he took the shot. True to basic human nature, he turned to see whence it came. Then the lights in the club went out, plunging every square inch into darkness except the office.

From out of the blackness, a blade soared through the air, finding its mark right in the very eye he'd winked at me. He dropped his assault rifle, wailing as he reached up to pull the blade free from his bloody socket.

Orlovsky fired his 45, raucous booms in succession, in the general direction of the throw. After a moment, he stopped and listened, unable to see if he'd hit anything. Probably as she had that day back in Boston when she wiped out his brother Leonid and most of his men, Joseline, thigh high boots and all, introduced herself in dramatic fashion. She'd dodged his random shots and dove out of the darkness and through the window opening where the spy glass once stood.

Before either of them could react, she went into a seamless tuck and roll before springing up and delivering a perfect kill shot into the one eyed man standing atop the desk. Dead before he even knew it, he collapsed right in front of us, extinguishing some vodka flames while eliciting another shrill shriek in my ear from Aimée.

"I told you to get Smith! What the fuck?" I asked Joseline as she took cover with us, squatting low as Orlovsky resumed shooting. I was so angry with her for disobeying me that I could kiss her. At least we had numbers in our favor now.

"I vowed to protect you and to finish this with Orlovsky. That other fuckboy Smith has nothing to do with me," she reasoned with a smirk as she yanked the pink wig from her head. "And besides, you waste a lot of ammo."

"Uh...you see all these bodies, right? I killed them with no help from you. I thought you said I was an 'okay' shot," I reminded her.

"I lied," she bantered as she let off a shot to keep Orlovsky at bay. *"You're cheating on me already? Who's your little friend?"*

"Aimée," the shivering blonde answered for herself, speaking some English as she relinquished her fetal position to join us in a crouch close to the smoldering desk.

Joseline nodded at her, shrugging as she tried to get a bead on the large, but quick man who resumed cursing in Russian. Having some backup now, I tried again to clear the jammed rifle to pull my weight.

Through the wall space where Joseline had made her entrance, I could see backup coming to his aid, red laser sights cautiously fanning out over the empty dance floor and heading our way.

"Strange," Joseline offered as she saw the same thing, now firing from behind the repurposed body of the man atop the desk. She shot twice at the new arrivals, sending them scurrying behind overturned club tables and chairs.

"What?" I asked her, almost done ejecting the jammed round and ready to help hold them at bay.

While keeping her gun trained toward the enemy, Joseline cut her eyes Aimée's way. There was something on her mind which I was missing.

"Metu," Joseline uttered; some gibberish I didn't understand.

"Nomini," the scared blonde spat almost immediately with an eerie smile, her demeanor changing from hysterical to deathly calm before I could even get a word out.

Just before she plunged a knife into Joseline.

32-Joseline

"You bitch!" I yelled, as she plunged a dagger deep into my trapezius muscle. She barely missed neatly severing my spine, but only because I sidestepped just as she made her move. If you know you can't avoid a wound, might as well determine the best outcome. She missed anything vital and it hurt like a thousand wasp stings, but the trick was not to give her another shot. Like I was taught, I blocked the pain and put off passing out for another time.

I had a hunch about this girl even though she was convincing as hell. But I wasn't sure until I saw her break character out the corner of my eye and gave her our traditional challenge to which she couldn't ignore. All of us in The Nest had different ways of deception. This one liked to play the "helpless damsel" with men, lulling them into a false sense of security until it was too late. Truth was good, but he was nowhere near one hundred percent on his game. She probably was about to poke him like a piñata if I hadn't come back.

And what did I get for my trouble?

I reached back and grabbed my Sister's hand, struggling to keep her from using the knife again. Every wiggle of it in my muscle nauseated me, but I was resolute in not dying yet, so she wasn't getting her knife back unless I was the one delivering it in her conniving heart. Orlovsky, who'd been biding his time toying with Truth, knew his woman had made her move, so he moved on us. But I still held on to my gun and squeezed off a shaky shot, wounding him as my Sister clawed at my eyes with her free hand.

Truth tried to get her off me, but she grabbed the dead man's rifle. No time to aim, she improvised and swung it like a club, cracking him upside the head with the buttstock. Knocked silly, he went cross-eyed, receiving a deep gash above his ear for his troubles. I hadn't sparred with one of my Sisters in years and seeing her speed from my end gave me pause and a brief bit of admiration even as she tried to kill us.

Truth's noble effort was enough though to distract her from the knife she was trying to retrieve from my back. Letting go of the knife in me as well as my gun, I reached back with both hands and grasped the back of her head. With a firm grip, I violently yanked her head forward over my shoulder and brought up my knee, delivering a sickening crunching sound as the bones in her face relented. As I was about to deliver another one and end this, machine gunfire dotted the desk, chewing it up as the red laser dots from Orlovsky's men came closer to locking on us.

Truth was still dazed from that rifle blow, but went full automatic, spraying cover fire out the office window to give them something to think about. While my Sister struggled through the tears, swelling eyes and broken nose I bestowed upon her; I pulled her blade out, wincing from the pain as I gnashed my teeth.

"Are you—," Truth began to ask.

"Go on! Finish him!" I urged Truth with a grunt as Orlovsky scooted backwards on his butt toward the office door, attempting a getaway. I'd wounded him in the side and he kept a hand pressed against his ribs, a red trail following him as he mopped the floor with his crawling body.

Truth jumped up to pursue through the smoky haze, but those red dots returned followed by another furious round of gunfire, their signature rat-a-tat-tat deafening in the small space. They intended on keeping us pinned down, away from their boss as he made his escape. The light I left on in here when I killed those in the club now had us at a disadvantage, mice in a brightly lit cage.

"Fuck!" Truth bellowed in frustration as his target slipped away before his eyes. For a moment, I thought he was going to charge headlong into a hail of bullets on some suicide run. But he wasn't totally mad...yet.

I went to instruct him to shoot out the lights overhead, but had more immediate concerns. While still on her back, my Sister kicked upward at me with her heel, striking my wrist then my jaw, jarring her stiletto blade from my hand in the process. After swinging her leg over, she came back with a sweeping kick which caught me on my temple. Pretty impressive to be that limber in such close quarters. Stunned, I fell over as she reached up to brace herself on the desk.

"You...you're the one who left us," the blonde I'd never met before tonight hissed, spitting out a tooth.

"I'm also the one who's going to kill you, Sister," I proclaimed as convincingly as I could.

She managed a smirk from her shattered face. Before my knee fucked her up, she was attractive in a slutty kind of way. Poor thing picked the wrong client to work for, but we all had our vows. They all took us to our graves, just some sooner than others.

I did a kip up, quickly springing back to my feet as she charged me. She assaulted me with a series of jabs and palm strikes from every angle, switching martial arts styles to confuse me. I defended well and blocked most of them as I retreated, but could only go so far lest I risk being hit by probing gunfire. Truth prepared to shoot her, but we were too close together in our game of death for him to risk it. Instead, he bum-rushed her, figuring to use his weight and size advantage, but she caught him in a Judo toss, slamming him onto his bum arm as she used his weakness to her advantage. As he grimaced and writhed in pain on the floor, she returned her focus to me.

Knowing her vision was messed up; I unleashed a spin kick into her ribs, breaking at least one of them. She groaned, but still caught my leg and held on for dear life. With all her might, she drove her bony elbow into the side of my knee. I hadn't a second to scream as she swept my other leg out from under me, sending my head banging against the floor.

I saw stars, but tried to scramble to my feet. My jammed knee gave though and I awkwardly tumbled over. My Sister regained her stiletto, waving it threateningly in front of her while propping herself on the smoldering desk. The menacing red laser dots danced on the wall just over my shoulder. With Truth down behind her, she planned to keep me pinned between her blade and their bullets.

"Come on then," I said as I stood proud. "I'd rather it be you than them."

Spitting blood out the side of her mouth, she prepared to make her move while I tried to figure out how much damage I could inflict before her knife wounds got the best of me. I braced myself for her assault. Her broken ribs hindered her though, so she placed a hand on the desk to push off.

But just as she leapt, Truth came out of nowhere and impaled her hand with his ceramic blade, pinning her to the desk. She howled like some wounded animal caught in a trap and tried to yank her hand free, wildly flailing at him with her dagger in the process. He dodged her frantic thrusts, but she forgot about me, intent on freeing herself. That sloppiness was her undoing.

I was behind her before she could react, one arm already wrapped around her throat. With my other hand, I grabbed her knife hand and forcibly shoved her own blade up under her jaw and into her skull. Her body shook and clung to that last bit of life, but I held onto her, humming into my Sister's ear to send her off as pleasantly as possible. "Metu Nomini Infinitus," I whispered in her honor when I sensed it was all over, regretting having never known her name.

Blood streaming down the side of his head, Truth stared at the hand he'd stabbed, noticing the same ancient owl brand between the fingers as mine.

"Wow," he muttered, eyes wide with the realization he'd survived something most don't.

I nodded, thanking him for his quick thinking, but our respite was already over. No longer worried about hitting my Sister or their boss, Orlovsky's men unleashed their full fury on the office, weapons on full automatic and spraying every square inch of the place as they finally advanced. More and more of our desk shelter was winnowed away and we clung as close together as we could, chunks of wall plaster and pictures falling almost literally onto our heads.

"What the fuck are we gonna do?" Truth wondered aloud as Orlovsky's men could be heard clambering through the opening into the office.

ERIC PETE

33-Truth

"I'm out of magic," I gasped at Joseline while blindly reaching up over my head to retrieve my blade from the dead woman's impaled hand. Released from her tether, the assassin's body lazily slid down onto the floor, keeping us company. "You?"

Joseline's reply was to yank the blonde's stiletto from her skull, leap up in the middle of a hail of gunfire and hurl the knife at them, striking and killing another one. Damn her efficiency. "Nope," she replied as she ducked down next to me again. "I got nothin'."

We checked our clips to see how many rounds remained between the two of us. The summation wasn't good as our mutual sighs revealed. Without exposing her head, she looked around from our limited vantage point, analyzing the bullet-riddled walls as well as the floor. There were no magic trap doors or secret wall panels; at least not on this side of the office. Joseline kept looking though, fixating on the shape of the room as if it revealed something.

"Traboules!" she blurted out in French before switching to English. "The passages!"

"What are you talking about?" I asked, wondering if the stress of killing her sister assassin had unhinged her.

"World War II," she began. "The Resistance had secret passages in a lot of these old buildings. You don't remember the blueprints?" she shouted, pointing at a tiny corner of the office to our right.

"Not really," I admitted as I popped up, shooting another one barely ten feet away. "I was more concerned with current doors 'n shit," I said as I made myself small again, squirming away from the blasts of gunfire now penetrating the desk as well as the blonde's body.

Our conversation and my history lesson would have to wait as they came at us again. In a twisted game of whack-a-mole, Joseline popped up on one end of the desk, firing her gun once. When they focused on where she had just been, I popped up on my end, unleashing automatic weapon spray which wounded two of them. It only enraged them more, curse words in guttural Russian raining our way as they dragged their men to safety. But Joseline popped up again, wounding or killing the two rescuers this time. I think they took it personal now.

"I'm out," she said, dropping the clip from her gun.

"Here. You can probably put this to better use than me," I said as I slid my assault rifle over, out of breath. They were going to throw caution to the wind eventually and I still had my blade in case they decided to get up close and personal. "Now what about the passages?"

"There's probably not a lot on the other side of that wall separating us from one," she mentioned, pointing emphatically toward that same corner again. We'd have to dodge a shit storm of bullets to make it there. Then somehow get through a fucking wall with no tools while avoiding being shot repeatedly in the back. But at least it was a plan.

Kinda.

We weren't allowed time to come up with anything else though. A clinking sound broke the silence followed by a "plink" as something bounced once off the wall before rolling into view.

"Grenade!" I yelled as the round object came to rest between us.

Joseline wasted not second as she took the assault rifle and used it like a golf club, swinging it at the grenade. She launched the grenade perfectly in the direction of the tiny wall, but we were still too close when it exploded.

The force of the blast bowled us over with the shockwave bursting blood vessels in my eyes, bloodying my nose and replacing my hearing with a constant ringing sound. I blinked several times, slowly daring to move my body, but it was hard to get anything to work right. Orlovsky's men paused to see if we were dead, assuming that we were amidst the dust and debris. Joseline acted on that, yanking me to my feet. She pulled me along as we stumbled toward the wall in the corner, now splintered and flimsy, but still there. Somehow we managed to run which is when the shots came, nipping at our heels then buzzing past our ringing ears. With the dust cloud obscuring us, Joseline aimed the assault rifle ahead and let it rip, using up the remaining ammo in an attempt to break through to a mysterious passage we prayed was there.

And on faith alone, we ran headlong into a wall.

Yes, a wall.

34-Truth

"Fuck," she cursed, discarding our last true weapon on the fly. Frantically running head-on, the wall ahead still looked pretty solid to me.

Despite feeling like I'd been run over by a truck, my body started to numb; the last bit of adrenaline helping me along. Blood pooled in my mouth and I suspected some internal damage from that grenade, but was too busy with that whole "stay alive" thing to dwell on it.

That blasted wall loomed closer and closer, either our salvation or a cruel joke and the end of the line. I at least wanted to look Orlovsky in the face, going out defiant as possible, when I died. But getting mowed down in the back by his men like some makeshift firing squad seemed more likely. Joseline was still resolute even in this crazy instance, so I used that to keep despair at bay one frenzied step at a time.

A shot caught Joseline in her arm, sending her spilling face first onto the floor as Orlovsky's men fired at will. It was time for me to take the lead and I hopped over her, grabbing her same injured arm to yank her along, not having time for niceties or apologies. A few stumbles and she was righted again, growling to psych herself up.

Before we went splat, I scanned for some sign of a hollow space ahead, but couldn't tell from the shadows or grenade damage if it existed. Then a few more shots strafed us, landing in the far left corner instead. I watched carefully as we were only a foot away with no second chance. Rather than ricocheting off brick or masonry this time, the shells just disappeared into the wall, leaving gaping black holes.

"There!" I emphasized with an extra tug on Joseline's arm in the scant seconds before impact. I twisted my body in that direction as hard as I could, using my remaining strength and last good shoulder to plow ahead. I felt the edge of a brick wall at first, jarring me, but as I kept pushing and rolled through, the space adjacent to it gave way. Joseline's momentum added to mine and we suddenly found ourselves plummeting through wooden boards and rusted pipes that scraped and ripped at us along every yielded inch. Before long, as the space seemed to shrink again, my face had become a battering ram. I'm not claustrophobic, but imagined this to be a horrible way to die, all Edgar Allen Poe in "The Cask of Amontillado" except pumped full of gunshots and left to rot. When it seemed there was no air to breathe and nowhere else to budge, we broke through.

Old bricks crumbled and relented as we burst through, tumbling over one another into a walkway with only the barest of ambient light shining through. The gunshots from the other side kept coming, but weren't reaching us...for now.

We'd emerged in one of those ancient passageways, probably unused since World War II. The air tasted heavy and damp, but we could breathe. Lying motionless on my back and with cobwebs clinging to my clothes, I allowed myself a half-cough half-laugh. Joseline crawled over and joined me, her toothy smile barely visible. Her dress had to be shredded.

"Abracadabra," I joked before she kissed me on my bloody lip. In our state, it wasn't very romantic; but mortar particles, dust and all; still rather enjoyable.

"Truth, can you move?" she asked, realizing her leaning on me might not the best idea.

"If you mean my dick, I don't think we're fucking right now," I dryly joked.

We helped one another to our feet, hearing muffled Russian voices too close for comfort. They'd stopped shooting and were seeking answers. Beyond that, we could hear police sirens and large numbers of people conversing in French, a pissed off Leonardo

DiCaprio possibly among them. We'd emerged somewhere near the outside of the club where police, stretched thin, were only now responding to the mayhem we'd orchestrated.

"We need to get patched up, lick our wounds and get some rest," Joseline said as we felt our way in the dark, wobbly legs barely working.

"No. Orlovsky," was all I uttered, stopping dead in my tracks. I imagine she could see my eyes.

"C'mon. Look at us. You can't be serious. We don't even know where he's at by now," she tried reasoning with me. She seemed frustrated and annoyed.

"Oh, but I do," I corrected her.

35-Truth

A fast-moving storm brewed outside; enough rain, wind and lightning to wash away the sins of the world. Or at least enough to put out a warehouse fire along the Rhone.

Speaking of sins, a rather large sinner limped along in the church using a makeshift cane for support. Unlike Saint-Serge-De-Radonege in Paris, there was a smaller Russian Orthodox church in Meyzieu, a little town east of Lyon. Lightning flashed and he stopped to stare at the illuminated three-beamed cross hovering over the altar and the painted dome above. In his other hand, he held a half empty bottle of vodka. While holding his gaze on the icons adorning the wall behind the altar, he seemed to mutter a prayer; maybe something to the effect of thanks for the round from Joseline's gun not being a few inches to the left. Beneath his loose shirt, the fresh bandages and wrap around his ribs were bulky.

Another flash of lightning cast a shadow, but that of a living being this time.

"I'm sorry for all the noise, Father Niklaus. And for my drinking," he apologized in Russian with a chuckle. "But it has been one hell of a night."

"I agree, Dimitri," I replied instead of the priest for whom he somehow mistook me. "You have a lot to be sorry for."

Orlovsky turned so quickly that he seemed to tear his sutures, hunching over in pain. I hadn't the time or want for such a luxury as stitches or bandages, still leaving bits of my blood and sweat wherever I stepped. "Why don't you die!" he cursed as he hurled the vodka bottle my way to clench his side. Luckily, it wasn't lit this time and rolled harmless at my feet.

"Because I'm a ghost. 'Chernyy Prizrak', right?" I taunted as I aimed the Ruger 9mm with the laser scope in the center of his forehead. No misses allowed this time. "Don't worry about your men outside. They're safely out the weather. Permanently."

"How did you find me?" he asked, hiding whatever he was really thinking.

"Patterns. I'm kinda good at seeing them," I chirped as I limped closer, still training my very own red dot on his head. Dude was massive though, so I was cautious not to get too close. After escaping his club, I only had time for a quick shower, change of clothes and another dose of pain pills. One arm had been useless since Paris, now all my other limbs were on borrowed time. My gun hand felt like limp spaghetti while the arm to which it was attached felt as heavy as the lead in the bullets. "Like there's always a Russian Orthodox church within twenty miles of the clubs where you frequent. I'll give it to you. You're smart to have your men keep a low key presence outside. Almost didn't see them. What's the deal, yo? A fascination with angels? Thinking about a change in careers?"

"Growing up back in Russia, the church was good to me and my brothers; especially when the Soviets were in charge. The church has continued to be good to me. Shelter...from the storm," he cracked in reference to the thunder clap that hit with perfect timing. The only reason he'd share that was because he knew one of us wouldn't be walking out of here alive.

"And you're a great benefactor, I'm sure," I surmised. "By the way, don't worry about Father Nicklaus. He's unharmed and won't see any of this."

"*You'd kill me in a church?*" he growled, trying to intimidate with his size. All I saw was a weak, flawed man who did his dirt then hid in the church at night like a scared little boy.

"Nah. I'm going to hell eventually, but it doesn't need to be that hot," I answered, surprisingly lowering my gun. "My mom's from New Orleans. She was raised a big time Catholic and would never forgive me if I killed you here," I stated as I sheepishly nodded my head at something else garnering my attention. "Now...my friend on the other hand..."

Orlovsky awkwardly craned his neck to see Joseline lurking in front the Beautiful Gate, the doors to the sanctuary which were used only by the Orthodox clergy. She was clergy of some sort; a seductive kung-fu ninja high priestess of swift and righteous vengeance.

"You killed Katya?" he asked her, his voice uncharacteristically softening while giving the true name of the crazy blonde who almost killed us all by her lonesome.

Joseline remained silent and didn't dignify him with an answer. Instead, she walked over and snatched his walking stick from his hand. I don't think he'd ever had a woman be that bold because he laughed as he hobbled in place. Joseline, emotionless in her expression, tilted her head to the side as she spun his sticking in her hand. When she stopped spinning it, she whipped it once between his legs, cracking him in the nuts. His laughter was replaced by him sucking air. She whipped the stick through the air again, coming down across his head with a "THWAP!"

36-Truth

"Did everything go as expected, Lieutenant Villeré?" I asked the head of the local Gendarmerie.

"Oui," he replied. "The men showed up at the hotel in Corbas like you said they would. Some resisted...like you said they would."

"Was there an American with them? Anyone matching the description I gave you?" I questioned, a bit apprehensive. When I sent Orlovsky's men running from the club on a wild goose chase, I was really sending them into a trap, using a local official I hoped wasn't on the take.

"No. I checked both the dead and the living. No one fits," the lieutenant replied. "I have to ask you. Do the warehouse explosion and the shootout at the discothèque have any connection to this? Because we were spread too thin last night to respond to the shootout in time. Would you know anything about this, my mysterious friend? Is it all connected?"

"Other than it being a bunch of Russians? Not that I'm aware of," I coyly answered. "Funny how some of your arrests match more than a few of the alleged Paris 'victims', huh?"

"Dimitri Orlovsky won't like this. Most of this involves his 'interests'. With these arrests, the entire precinct is...apprehensive," the lieutenant admitted, a bit of trepidation in his voice.

"That is why I provided the intel to you," I stated. "You seem like a man who cares about what goes on in his country. They'll probably promote you to Capitaine. As for Orlovsky, don't worry about him."

"Should I ask?" he sighed.

"And keep me on the phone longer so this call can be triangulated? Adieu, Inspector," I said as I hung up my satellite phone. Joseline, who'd been checking her watch, gave me a thumbs-up.

"Staaaaay schemin'," she sang, mimicking the hook to that Rick Ross song. A few hours of sleep, some makeshift medical attention and French onion soup had returned her color. "Mr. Smith?" she asked about Piatkowski.

"Gone," I replied, pretending it didn't concern me. "But we do have something for our troubles," I offered as I hit the remote in my pocket. The trunk of the old car where we were standing popped open. As we stared at the cargo in back, a soccer ball rolled into our feet on the dusty, hard ground.

"Qui est-il?" the little boy asked. His father was a Sudanese immigrant who ran this junkyard.

"Just a silly white man," I replied in French. "Go. Tell you father we're almost ready," I said as I handed him one hundred Euros. He skipped away, kicking his soccer ball as he went along.

Orlovsky squinted as his eyes adjusted to the light. I removed the gag from his mouth, but still left him bound. Joseline took even less of a chance and kept a gun aimed at him. She'd argued in favor of her more direct method the entire drive.

"I'm not a very good killer," I admitted, leaning in so the Russian boss could hear me. "But congratulations. You've given me an appreciation for it."

"Then why am I still alive? You're going to hold me for ransom? Or to catch Piatkowski?" he reasoned, a large lump on his forehead still present as well as the black eye Joseline had delivered for good measure.

"No. Neither of those. Piatkowski will be dealt with. And you are of no importance," I said as I stood back up and rested my hand on the trunk lid. "What you see now. The predicament you find yourself in? This is what I do best. Punish. Make people feel regret and sorrow. Sow misery."

"You are sick," he nervously laughed.

"Yep," I nodded in agreement. "And you killed my friend. You made it extremely personal when you did that in Paris. Plus you killed innocent civilians. I usually get revenge for others, but today, I'm feasting at the table."

"My men will find you. They won't stop looking for me and they will find you," he stressed, his voice wavering some.

"No they won't, Dimitri. Most of them have been taken care of. Nature abhors a vacuum and you're not as important as you think. Those of your men who remain will slide right into your role and you'll be forgotten. You want to be remembered. You need to be remembered. But you won't be."

"Wait. We can start over. I'll… I'll deliver Piatkowski to you. I'll give you money. I have lots of it," he pleaded.

"You're gonna die in this trunk in this junk yard with all the other forgotten scraps and no one will find you. Just you alone with your screams because no one will hear you and nobody is coming. Ever. And you know what's ironic? I'm gonna leave the keys to this trunk and your salvation out here. Just outside of your reach," I informed him, dangling the keys before I tossed them over my shoulder.

"Not like this! Nyet! Nyet! Nyet!" he yelled as he squirmed to free himself, the cold reality of it all setting in. Joseline's gun kept him somewhat in check.

"Your brothers made a fatal mistake years ago in Boston by fucking with us. Now you have committed the same mistake. Goodbye, Dimitri Grigorevich Orlovsky," I said as I slammed the trunk shut.

"You sure he doesn't have another brother? Or a sister? Because if so, we need to just go put a bullet in their head now," Joseline muttered.

"No, I'm sure. He's the last one," I assured her. "You are free and clear."

I nodded to the junkyard owner who stood next to the controls of the hydraulic car crusher in which the old Renault with Orlovsky sat. He flipped the switch.

"Why'd you lie to him about just leaving him here to rot?" Joseline asked me as the hydraulic compactor, true to its name, began closing down on the car as it were a fly in the grip of a monstrous Venus flytrap.

"It's what I do. I wanted to give him hope before he realized it was hopeless," I replied as I relished Orlovsky's panic, his screams barely audible over the loud mechanical ruckus. By the time the old car was mashed and flattened to a barely recognizable metal wafer, I imagined his last minutes of life to have been terrifying. It had to be final for Orlovsky. I couldn't risk him popping up years from now to torment me like Piatkowski.

"What now, Truth?" Joseline asked as we left the junkyard, muffled cries of fear and rage extinguished and in our rearview mirror. I curiously eyed her for a moment.

"Dinner. I am starving," I admitted, still hobbled and banged up, yet invigorated. "But let's get out of France first. I think we've worn out our welcome here."

37-Joseline

We boarded an unmarked plane out of Europe, flying south over the Mediterranean then the Atlantic. The large airliner only had about seven other passengers, but they all kept to themselves. No one asked questions beyond the basic niceties from the flight attendants who were absent nametags on their uniforms.

"Poor rating on Travelocity or something? Should I be concerned?" I asked Truth as nobody made eye contact nor seemed to care about the plethora of empty seats separating us.

"No. We're spaced apart like this on purpose. We don't know who they are and vice versa," he replied as he patted me on my arm. "It's meant to provide privacy and discretion, but seems like just any other major airline to air traffic control. Get some rest. You are in good hands."

At ease, I smiled and placed my head on his shoulder, ignoring the throbbing pain beneath the fresh bandages on my back and arm. For better or worse, I'd developed a fondness and trust for this wily chameleon with the forked tongue. I guess I just had a craving for danger.

We touched down on an isolated runway before dawn, somewhere in the Eastern Hemisphere, probably North Africa by the land features and look of the grounds crew. All the passengers either had private SUVs waiting for them or smaller planes to board, nobody bothering to look back as they disembarked. Truth and I hustled onto a Cessna CJ4 he'd arranged then continued on our journey. We landed somewhere in South Africa probably around noon, taking a small cab from that point on. The cabbie questioned us, guessing we were a famous couple or something. I let my partner indulge him while I just smiled and nodded my head. If the poor guy only knew how far off he was and what we were really about, he'd probably piss all over himself. At the end of the drive, Truth paid the man in rand outside some house in a residential neighborhood near the coast.

"Um...why are we in Capetown?" I asked Truth, my yawn from the long flight ending with my mouth agape. "Piatkowski's somewhere nearby? Is this a weapons cache of yours?"

"C'mon," was all he said as he opened a door to the white, cube-shaped abode and led me in. "There's a view of the Twelve Apostles Mountains. And the Atlantic over there," he said as he limped across the main floor of the three story villa, pointing as he went along. Outside the floor-to-ceiling windows and beyond the outdoor deck was a sight fit for a postcard. "You've got your own room, complete with wardrobe. It's the master suite. Oh. There's a maid too. She picked out your clothes per the measurements I gave her. If something doesn't fit, it's on me. Put a bullet in my head. She's too sweet to terrorize."

"Why are we here?" I asked again.

"As far as anyone here knows, we're just a rich Silicon Valley couple who had a bad safari experience when our vehicle rolled over. I figure you deserve some drama-free downtime minus unnecessary questions," Truth replied as he opened the fully-stocked fridge and grabbed two bottles of Valpré spring water, tossing one to me underhanded.

"Okay. Thank you," I stated as I took my first gulp. "But why this place?"

Truth closed the fridge and walked my way, leaving his water unopened on the marble kitchen island. "Back in Orlovsky's club when you asked me if I could pick somewhere else to be," he began.

"Yeah," I said with a wide smile, pleased that he remembered that moment we shared even if it was borne of desperation.

"Well, this is it. I've owned this place for some time, but never told anyone; not even my friend Sophia. I only spent one night here before. I was afraid of jinxing it or enemies discovering it, like what happened to all my stuff stateside. This is going to be a spot for when I fully quit doing what I do... If I live long enough to enjoy it."

"And you brought me here," I softly mumbled to myself, admiring the panoramic view of Camps Bay below and the mountains above framed outside the windows. I felt a little something soft and mushy in my heart; probably random gas.

"Yeah," he replied, nervously scratching his head and wriggling his other arm in the sling. "I figure I trust you enough to share something like this. Over the past week or so, you've saved my ass countless times. It would be rude of me to not say 'Thank you'. This is my way of doing that."

"And that's your only reason?" I pushed as I glided his way across the teak hardwood floor.

"We're both pretty banged up. You can stay as long as you want. Heal your mind and body," he answered without really answering.

"And what about *your* mind and body, Truth? Are you going to let someone finally look at that arm and maybe get it set right? Because you can only pop so much pain medication before it takes you somewhere you don't want to go," I lectured him from experience.

"Not now. Maybe later," he said with an odd grin. He grabbed a remote and put on some music, piano keys and horns in concert. It was Andile

Yenana's "Wicked Whisper" I believe, based on my time in many a jazz bar around the world.

"Uh huh. Later because you're still going after Piatkowski," I accused him, not letting the pleasant musical arrangement distract me.

"He got away, but he can wait for now. He's missing Orlovsky's backing and muscle. I'll find him when I'm ready," Truth explained as he began to unbutton his shirt, not without some difficulty. Maybe this was a rest stop on his road to vengeance, but I wasn't fully convinced about our reasons for being here. "You're totally safe here. Get comfortable. We'll grab some dinner later," he said as he retired to one of the many rooms in the pristine house.

Without much trouble, I found the master suite waiting for me on the second floor. A hot tub was visible on the wooden deck just outside the sliding glass wall, but within a ten foot high privacy wall, away from neighbors' prying eyes. Smiling to myself, I fell back onto the king-sized bed like I was a kid. I didn't feel too young or innocent though as my knife and gunshot wounds reminded me, generating a sharp pain which made me wince. I gritted my teeth and got back up, prying myself from my wrinkled travel clothes which I left in a tiny heap on the bedroom floor.

I shuffled to the walk-in closet, turning on the light to see. "Whoa," I gasped at the wardrobe consisting of some of the most beautiful pieces upon which I'd ever laid my eyes, but I was more in need of a bath and quickly turned off the light.

Inside the bathroom, I ran the large free standing tub shaped like the lower half of an egg, adding lavender to the water flowing from the chrome faucet. I lit the scented candles on hand, ready to dim the lights and center myself with some meditation. But before doing that, I gazed at myself closely in the mirror, taking inventory. The scratches on my face would heal with time and cocoa butter; my swollen jaw would go away with some ice. I slowly swiveled my nude body, sizing up in the mirror how the rest of me fared at the Battle of Lyon. Wounds, both old and new, formed a tapestry of my life. Somehow, my tale wasn't complete. My fresh bandages weren't so fresh after our trip; instead a shade of pink as I pulled them off with a grimace and dumped them in the garbage can. Later on, I would burn them, sure to leave no trace of me. Finally, I pinned my hair up and did another quick in the mirror. "Yep. Still fine," I defiantly reminded myself as I slapped my own ass. A man once said I reminded him of a thicker, more chocolate Zoe Saldana, but I always fancied myself a more athletic Rosario Dawson.

I dimmed the lights then stepped into the tub, sliding down into the soothing, scented waters. It was a bit hot for some, but I liked it hot, welcoming the stings across my body as if I'd won another challenge. Deeply inhaling the lavender, I let my cares soak away and finally relaxed since Truth uncovered my hiding spot in Louisiana. I hated him at the time for it, but being so close to death these past days reminded me what living was really about.

I must've drifted off because I found myself in the D.R. at that bus stop in Azua, back when I was a small child. Mi madre and mi padre were arguing, as was usual, but I just wanted some candy from the store next door. After asking them again, they still ignored me. My father put his hand in my mother's face and she slapped it away. I still wanted a yaniqueque from the street vendor so badly, but now the bus was coming to take us to mi abuela in Santo Domingo. It was now or never and I ran toward the delicious rows of fried crispy treats on display, intent on snatching just one for our journey. Just as I moved, an old truck suddenly lost control. It came from across the street and barreled into the crowded bus stop, running over my parents and plowing into several others. Little Me opened her mouth to scream, same as always.

"Hey," a voice calmly called out instead.

I opened my eyes in surprise, reaching up and snatching Truth's wrist as I sent water splashing everywhere.

"Ow. You were having a bad dream," he said, revealing only a sponge in his hand. "Can I at least keep this hand?"

"Sorry," I remarked, embarrassed as I let go. Truth had cleaned up rather nicely, sporting a Nike white shirt and blue warmup pants with his bum arm more comfortably situated in a fresh sling. The subsiding bruises and faint scratches on his brown skin only made him look more rugged. He was more warrior than he cared to admit.

"May I?" he asked as he lowered the natural sponge in the still warm bath water.

Resuming my breathing, I nodded. "Did...did I say anything?" I asked as he squeezed the sponge over my shoulders, sending water running down the tops of my breasts.

"You were mumbling...in Spanish. But I didn't catch what you were saying. I just came in here looking for you," Truth replied as he began to bathe me, gently navigating over my wounds with the sponge.

"Peeping Tom," I joked as I let him tend to me, storing away that haunting memory for another time...as usual. It always returned as well as what happened after they died.

"Shit, I don't peep," he boasted as he rubbed my neck, eliciting a moan from me. "My eyes were wide open. Just as they are now."

I leaned forward in the tub, exposing my back and the top of my hips to him. With a deliberate sensual pace, he dragged the sponge down my spine, ending at the small of my back. Once there, he applied pressure, giving me goosebumps all over. My nipples responded, emerging above the surface of the water and hardening even more from the slight chill in the air. I bit my lip, pretending all was still calm inside me.

Truth went below the water, the sponge traveling over my hips before tracing along the outside of my thigh as he moved along the stone white tub, his eyes never leaving me.

"I can only imagine if you had both your hands free," I cracked with a wink as I leaned back into the waters. Arching my back, I gripped the sides of the tub then raised my legs up, playfully dancing in them the air for him.

"I'm learning to make do," he commented as he watched me twirl them around like a synchronized swimmer. Knowing he was *disabled*, I wrapped one leg around his neck and held him in place. With my other one, I playfully dragged my toe against his ear. He caught my foot, showering kisses on my ankle before moving up where he put my foot in his mouth, greedily sucking my toes. I always burned hot and that right there unleashed a gush from me, both legs quivering as I gasped.

Toying with him, I relinquished my hold and pulled my foot free of his wanton lips and tongue, pressing against his chest to keep him at bay. He pushed back against my foot, sliding his hand down my calf to my inner my thigh. I relented as his hand vanished beneath the water.

My breathing turned shallow as his hand swam between my legs. His knuckles barely grazed my labia before his thumb stopped at my clit.

"Si, papi. Touch it. Touch that shit, baby," I panted as his thumb nestled against it at just the right pressure. I felt my next release build as two fingers slipped in and out of my pussy, the water adding to the sensation. As he massaged my clit with his thumb, his pinky slipped down to my asshole, making me convulse and splash about as he probed around it. Almost growling, I nudged against his digits, wanting a whole lot more than gentle titillation.

"Are you about to cum?" he asked, licking his lips as his pinky slid inside my anus and wriggling around. His thumb pressed harder against my clit, two fingers now deep in my pussy.

"Yes, yes," I cried, my face almost beneath the water as I squirmed about on his hand. "Do it. Make this pussy cum."

Lubricated by me and the bath, his fingers writhed about in my openings, squishing sounds abound from the pool of pleasure. As I clenched him, my whole body tensed. Chills formed all over and my muscles locked up before that moment of orgasm.

Then it arrived; achieved with my erupting as he delivered me.

But the doorbell rang as my body spasmed about.

"I have to get that," Truth said, abruptly halting our fun.

"Wha...huh?" I mumbled, laboring heavily in the tub as he disappeared from sight, abandoning me to run to the door. After a moment, I righted myself then climbed out. "Well this is pretty fucked up," I muttered aloud as I hustled to the closet to find a robe, pussy throbbing and water still dripping off me.

I shuffled along, hearing Truth at the front door speaking with someone. As I tightened my robe, I detoured to the kitchen and chose a pretty sharp carving knife. Whoever ruined my moment was gonna get sliced like a turkey if they came here with bad intentions.

As I came upon him, Truth saw the knife in my hand. He looked spooked.

"Who are you talking to?" I asked, clenching the handle.

No matter how good the magic fingers, trust no man.

Especially one like him.

ERIC PETE

38-Joseline

"Who are you talking to?" I asked Truth, unable to see who or how many stood on the other side of that door.

"Him," he replied as he saw the look in my eyes, swinging the door open for me to see.

"Oh," I gasped at the sight of the pizza delivery guy balancing six boxes in the doorway while Truth tried to pay him.

"Can you give me a hand?" Truth asked me, wiggling his hand in the sling. "I mean...since you're here."

"Of...of course," I stuttered at which time he addressed the carving knife in my hand with a *"What the fuck?"* expression.

"Miss, you have a knife in your hand," the nervous delivery driver noticed too.

"She just likes to cut the pizza herself," Truth lied with a shrug and a grin, always quick on his feet.

"Honey, put that down and take those pizzas from the man so I can pay him."

After shutting the door, Truth trailed me to the kitchen, grinning all the way. The poor delivery driver earned his tip more than he knew, but Truth was wrong for leaving me in the lurch post-orgasm in the tub like that.

"You really were about to stab the little Afrikaner? Now you know this country ain't been outta Apartheid that long, Joseline," he taunted, his casual swagger shining absent any disguise.

"Ha. Ha. You got me," I remarked, all frowned up as I placed the warm boxes of pizza atop the island. "But what is this about?"

"You like pizza, right?"

"Well...yeah. But how do you know?" I replied, perplexed.

"On the flight, you mumbled something in your sleep about pizza. You didn't say what kind, so I ordered one of each from the pizzeria down the hill. I was supposed to be waiting for them, but kinda lost track," he remarked with a wicked smile while sniffing the remnants of me still on his fingertips.

"Wow. This is so very thoughtful," I gushed over the pizza gesture while shaking my head at his crudeness.

"I know you got dessert before dinner, but...," he teased as he opened the lids in sequence as if on a game show, exposing: pepperoni, vegetarian, five cheese, Mediterranean, Margherita and Hawaiian.

"Who said dessert was over?" I corrected him as I chose a slice of vegetarian. "Those magic fingers got me craving something a little more substantial. Well...after this pizza."

"Touché," he relented.

"It's good?" he asked as I chomped down.

"Mmmmm. Mmm hmm," I offered between chews as melted cheese trailed down my mouth, wondering if this is what a stay-at-home date night with bae would be like.

Truth uncorked a few bottles of chilled red wine from his digital cellar then joined me, partaking of way too many slices and probably too many drinks. Here, all the way across the ocean from America, he found a late 80s/ early 90s R&B and hip-hop station and cranked it up.

That night, we danced on the patio beneath the stars, numb to our battle scars as we limped and hobbled around, filled with laughter for no reason other than it felt good. I didn't even bother changing out of the bath robe, hugging Truth tight as he gripped our third or fourth bottle of wine which he chugged from time to time.

"Baby, don't you want to wrap that other arm around...this?" I slurred with a sashay, granting him a clear view of the slit in the robe. "We can have a real doctor come by here and take another look at it."

"When I'm ready," he calmly stated. "This is my penance for letting so many people down."

"Didn't know you were a masochist," I teased. "Should I check your back for self-flagellation?"

"You can check every mark on my body. But, spoiler alert, none of them are self-inflicted. I keep those up here in my head," he slurred as we spun around to Prince's "Adore". After a stumble of mine where we almost fell, we slowed it down a bit and took a seat.

"I've been rolling solo for so long since leaving The Nest. I missed being able to openly share what I do for a living. No one could handle it," I randomly blurted out, studying the ocean below and stars above.

"Now, that I can understand. When Collette back in Dallas...," he began, his voice drifting off.

"That girl whose husband's hand I whacked?" I asked, rudely reenacting the motion. Fuck it. I was drunk. Besides, he was about to kill Truth.

"Yeah. When you saved my life the first time. Her...his wife," he struggled to complete as he took another swig of wine, squinting at me. I yanked the bottle from him and drank as well. "When she found out about me, about what I really was, it was nothing nice."

"Wolves scare sheep," I mumbled as I passed the wine back, reminiscing on my first lesson learned as a frightened child on the road to becoming an assassin.

"Is that what we are? Wolves?" he grinned, his finger tapping on the neck of the bottle as he stood up.

"Si," I answered in my true accent and first language. "Gran lobos malo."

"Evil. Hot. I can get with it," he commented, the imprint of his eggplant in his warmups monopolizing my thoughts and making me wet. "So what now?"

"Time for some more dessert," I said with a rude, drunken burp as I reached for his pants and pulled them down. His erect shaft was almost staring me in the eye, daring me. I drunkenly winked back at it and smiled as I took hold. I welcomed him in my mouth, sloppily gagging on his manhood as though it were a Popsicle on hot day. Neighbors could've been watching, but neither one of us was bashful. Hide yo kids because grown folks was afoot.

"Damn that's good," Truth moaned as I lazily looped my tongue around his head then went deep, taking his length in my mouth before releasing with a "pop" from my lips. I repeated it over and over, drinking deeply of his dick just as he did the wine. Freeing my hands, I undid my robe, letting it fall away.

I exposed myself to Truth, cupping my breasts and spreading my legs for him. He looked on as I sucked him, his curled lips trembling as he muttered to himself. As I reached up and tenderly fondled his balls, he wobbled, but regained his footing.

"Your legs gonna last?" I said as I gripped his dick. Truth dropped the bottle right there, its last remaining contents spilling onto the deck as it rolled away.

"I'm still standing. Wanna test 'em?" he challenged with a smirk.

"Sure do," I said as I marched over to the balcony rail, my body commanding his attention. The stiff breeze coming off the ocean hardened my nipples like juicy brown pebbles. I clenched the rail and widened my stance. I flexed my ass cheeks and glanced back at him all demure, my timid eyes appealing to his manhood. "I need you to come take me. Right here," I called out as the stars twinkled overhead.

I'd worked him up good and Truth didn't hesitate. He pressed his body against mine, the heat from his crotch welcome. His tortured, ragged breath on my neck was almost as intoxicating as the wine. He clasped my waist with his calloused hand and slowly eased inside me, the dick making me bite my lip. I stood on my tiptoes and jutted my ass out, an involuntary tremor going through my body and my thighs quivering, a rare moment of vulnerability.

"That's it. Fill me up," I panted as he bit my ear lobe and nipped at my neck. Truth startled me with a sudden thrust, eliciting that welcome slapping sound between our bodies. The harder he fucked me from the back, the wilder my lust became. I came repeatedly, the sweet, sticky dampness connecting our bodies only heightening the moment of each orgasm.

"I've wanted you since Boston," he admitted in a guttural growl as he moved his hand across my stomach and over my breasts before inserting a finger in my mouth. I sucked it and playfully bit down before leaning back and kissing him, offering up my tongue.

Grinding on one another, my eyes rolled back just as one of the neighbors turned on the light and entered his kitchen. The elderly man stopped mid-reach at his cabinet, stunned to see the two of us fucking just outside his window.

"Truth...the neighbor," I gasped as he played with my nipples, squeezing them like plump grapes. I wheezed and came again all over his dick.

"He wishes he felt what I feel right now," Truth lazily sang in my ear as he continued his steady pump in and out. "Look at him. He wishes he had a woman such as you at least once in his life."

I gazed at the neighbor again, grinning as he nervously fidgeted in place. I found myself even more aroused as the kitchen suddenly went dark. "You have this pussy. He doesn't. Show him what you do with it, Truth," I begged, my eyes fixated on the dark window next door.

I fought back against his strokes with a rhythm of my own; made him work for it as I coaxed him along. I danced in Truth's head figuratively while dancing on his other head literally, my body equally adept at giving life as taking it. "I... I," he stuttered with a twitch, his sweaty body surrendering to me.

"That's it. Make me happy, boy," I cooed as he sped up. I worked my ass cheeks, clinging to each stroke as I summoned his seed. He held on to me with his good hand, almost lifting me aloft in our passionate exchange. After all we'd been through and how much he'd experienced at his enemies' hands, his stamina was impressive. But we'd won and he deserved a brief exorcism of his troubles as much as I desired getting my freak on.

Another shudder between our bodies and we'd arrived. I wildly whipped my head, tossing my hair across his face, and arched my back a final time. Truth froze in that moment where time stands still then erupted, joining his essence with mine as he clung dearly to me. We remained at the railing, leaning on it for support as our naked bodies weakly went through the motions to which they'd quickly become accustomed. As the pumping subsided, our heavy breathing remained, now in sync. While my pussy ached, I already longed for more. The night was young though and we had more locations and positions to try.

∞

"Truth?" I uttered, emerging from a stupor. My eyes were heavy and my thoughts cloudy. I awoke to an empty bed and the aroma of someone throwing down in the kitchen. The smells revitalized me as my stomach growled.

Laboring to move, I gathered myself and staggered over wrinkled sheets on my way to the bathroom. After taking a quick shower and pinning my hair up, I reapplied my bandages and found suitable clothes.

I found Truth cooking away on the stove top, his back turned to me and humming as if a huge burden no longer troubled him.

"How long was I asleep?" I asked him as my eyes struggled to adjust to the sunlight. I know it didn't fit with the décor, but this place could've used some curtains or blinds just then; maybe just a woman's touch to soften it up some.

"Twenty-four hours, give or take a day or so," he joked, freshly shaved and looking no worse for the wear. "I sent the maid away and trudged down the hill to snag some stuff at the market. I hope you like KingKlip. I pan-seared it with some peppers and spinach and gonna serve it on a bed of wild rice."

"Fucking and feeding me? A girl could get spoiled," I teased as my stomach growled more loudly this time.

"All part of being a good host," he remarked.

We ate at the kitchen counter, forgoing the wine and quickly scarfing down the meal. I think I really slept an entire day. But how long did he sleep? And what did he do with his time?

"Want to go into town? Maybe down to the beach?" I asked, smiling warmly from our drunken night of fun as I looked forward to a repeat...minus the whole drinking and voyeur neighbor part.

"No. I've got a job for you that requires your immediate attention," he replied coolly, acting as if all were just business between us. "It pays one mil American. Easy job for you."

"Huh? Why?" I simply asked.

"Because it pays. And it's what you do. You are a wolf, right?" he reminded me as he slid a scrap of paper across the table; one on which two names and addresses were scribbled. "Two kills...in New Orleans. All the information's there. If you care to, you can ride the street car afterwards and get a po-boy or something. Or maybe drive up I-10 and check on your boyfriend and his little girl. I'm sure she'd like to see you again."

I read the information then balled the paper up, tossing it in his face. My pussy suddenly no longer ached for him.

"Can you handle it?" he followed up, having the nerve to be perturbed.

"Of course," I replied just as clinical as he. "Are you coming with me?" I asked, already knowing the answer.

"No," he said as he took our plates and began rinsing them in the sink. That fork would go well in his eye.

"Will you be here when I return?" I followed up, wanting him to be what he was and not this stranger. Had he played me this whole time?

"No. But the place is yours. As long as you like," he offered, slightly warmer than his previous words. It only seemed to make him more of a jerk though.

Lashing out, I leapt over the counter and punched him upside his head. He fell hard onto the pristine kitchen floor, blinking his eyes to shake it off. I stepped over him, making sure to walk atop his hurt arm. "Asshole," I spat as I left for America, hoping to never see him again.

ERIC PETE

39

Chavanoz-French countryside

He sat hunched over in the corner of the café, his back to a wall and scrutinizing the tiny storefront for anybody that might be looking for him. And they were certainly looking for him. Before resurfacing, he was already wanted for misappropriating CIA funds and going on the run...allegedly, but now had the association with Orlovsky added to his WANTED bio.

"Monsieur, would you like another espresso?" the waiter asked as he removed Piatkowski's plate from the table, scraping up the crumbs as well.

"Oui," he replied still damp and shivering from exposure. The past twenty-four hours hadn't been very good to him.

Piatkowski barely escaped the police trap in Corbas, ducking into a bathroom when he spotted an undercover policeman. It wasn't hard for him. After all, he was on the side of law enforcement most of his life and had used the very same tactics. At least until the man Orlovsky referred to as "the Black Ghost" turned it all upside down for him. The same person responsible for the set-up he barely avoided, no doubt. He was either fortunate or unfortunate for the storm that came through, chilling him to the bone while also covering his escape. From the gunfire he heard, he knew most of the men with him at the hotel were dead or in the hospital. If he dared return to Orlovsky, he was as sure as dead too.

But somehow he knew Orlovsky was no longer a threat to anyone in this life.

Beyond the runny nose, Piatkowski felt a deep ache in his bones. Was he coming down with pneumonia? Would he die a fugitive in a country of socialized medicine and moody America-haters? Maybe his adversary was better than he. Maybe he should've left well enough alone when freed from that dungeon. Right now, he'd gladly settle for suburban Virginia and its humdrum simplicity.

He'd responded to the urgent message left on his voicemail by calling back, simply leaving the number to his new burner phone. Were they ever going to return his call? He rotated the phone on the table, spinning it like hands on a clock every few seconds. Maybe Interpol or somebody back home had already compromised it. Maybe he should ditch it already.

"Monsieur, your espresso," the waiter advised as he returned with the hot cup. Piatkowski took a quick sip then thanked him, deciding he'd stayed in one spot for too long. As he exited the café, his phone finally rang.

"Baby?" he hastily answered as he walked beneath an awning and stopped.

"Where the fuck you been, Nate?" Ronnie yelled.

"Busy, trying to take care of our problem, remember?" he replied, her threats of keeping his son away from him fresh on his mind. "Is everything okay?"

"No, it's not!" she replied, her volume still assaulting his ear.

"What's wrong? Do you need some cash?" he suggested.

"I told you I don't need your money. I need my life!" she answered.

"What are you talking about?"

"Ezell's dead, Nate!" Ronnie screamed, referring to her right hand man. "He killed him! And he's threatening to kill me and little Nate next."

"Wait, wait. That doesn't make sense. He threatened my wife and son last time, but that was all talk. Just a bunch of lies to get to me."

"Well, I guess you done pissed him off now, genius," she muttered. "You guaranteed you'd kill him; except you didn't!"

"How...how do you know he killed Ezell?" he asked the mother of his sole living child, trying to rationalize things. "I mean... New Orleans can be a dangerous place. And your family has enemies."

"Because he left a fuckin' note carved into Ezell's body. That's how I know," Veronica murmured. Her tone alarmed him more than anything because Ron DMC was afraid of no man, not even him. "Lawd, he did my boy wrong. Left him naked on the roof of his car with his dick cut off and shoved in his mouth, Nate. Ezell ain't no pig. They just evil."

"Do...do you know what the note says?" he asked her, trying to scour that image of Ezell from his mind.

"I got a partna in NOPD. He snapped a photo of it and sent it to me. It's a bunch of numbers plus a date followed by the message to come alone," she reported, her normally defiant voice wavering.

Piatkowski had the woman he considered his girlfriend and lifeline recite the numbers to him; quickly realizing they were coordinates with the accompanying date only two days away. His brow furrowed as he tried to place the location in his head. "Okay. I got it," he coolly uttered while screaming on the inside.

"You better. You failed yo wife and first kid. Handle yo business and kill this nigga, Nate. Be a man and protect your family before we're gone too," Ronnie ended.

He paused a moment, contemplating Ronnie and little Nate slaughtered and put on display like Ezell. He attempted to fathom ever so slightly if he could live with himself after allowing such a thing. Ronnie could be the ultimate bitch and any dreams of decency had long since bled away, but she was right. He had to be a man and protect his last semblance of family.

Piatkowski dropped the cell phone and crushed it beneath his heel.

40-Truth

Soweto, South Africa

(Latitude: -26,2533, Longitude: 27,9250)

I shaded my eyes, staring up toward the twin Orlando Towers, a sky bridge spanning the open air between them. The large cooling towers were a remnant of an old power plant, but revitalized with brightly painted murals, they now served as the main attraction for bungee jumps and other extreme sports. A good job repurposing a potential eyesore, but I had the center closed for the day over a suspect safety violation. That left my one-man inspection team with free rein of the place today and today only.

"They come," my walkie-talkie squawked once, my eyes in the township alerting me as my guest crossed the boundary I'd set up. If I'd just killed Piatkowski myself years ago, none of this would've happened. Instead, I was waiting for our final showdown with one arm in a sling. At least he got my message loud and clear.

As the old van approached, dust flew in its wake. I clenched and released my free hand, breathing deeply as so many memories over the years flashed through my head. I was out of fancy and intricate schemes and just wanted to see my tormentor eye-to-eye in the end.

But as the van stopped, I was reminded that things never go that easy. He arrived with company, four angry customers armed with the usual equipment-an assortment of handguns and Uzis. I presumed they were Orlovsky loyalists he'd somehow wrangled into helping him. I could've fled into the adventure park and evaded them, but that meant Piatkowski perhaps escaping again. I was sick and tired of the games. Nope, this was the end of the road.

"I said to come alone," I called out to the smaller man in the middle of four black bedecked Russians as they cautiously trod across the grass field. Maybe I should've planted landmines.

"I was, but then I found a few friends who want to party," he taunted.

"You must not care about Veronica or your boy back in New Orleans after all," I remarked.

"Thing is, I told her to get somewhere safe and you're not gonna be able to call anyone to do anything to them. I got all cell reception jammed from the moment we drove up," Piatkowski said as he pointed to his head with a smirk. He probably had jamming equipment in the van.

"Then you better stop right there," I as I pointed my nine millimeter in their direction. "Unless you want to blow up before me and you get to have our 'quality time'."

"Booby-traps?" he asked, maybe believing me as he stopped walking immediately. The other four fanned out to cover more ground and give me less of a target, but moved much slower now. "Some of us will make it through. And since you were stupid enough to go 'lone-wolf', I guess we win."

"Suit yourself," I shrugged, figuring I might as well start shooting while I had a chance. Maybe I could eliminate one or two before they cut me down. But something in the knee length grass gave them pause. One mumbled something in Russian to the others, but before they could reply, it was upon them. "What the fuck!" Piatkowski yelled in a panic, his accusing eyes glaring at me as he assumed this was my doing. The hooded figure had been camouflaged, lurking in the grass the whole time, surprising even me.

Joseline? I thought for a split second, but knew it couldn't be her. She was an ocean away in NOLA. I almost shot at them, but they weren't interested in me...for now. They unsheathed a curved sword, and it wasn't for show either. With a single upstroke, one of the men was slit from his nuts to his neck, gutting him like a lab specimen. The man closest to him yelled, but was immediately silenced, cleanly beheaded in one fluid swing. The other two immediately converged on the stranger with one of them firing their handgun, but the stranger sidestepped the shots and spun around, planting the long blade into the Russian rushing up from behind. As they planted a foot against the Russian's chest and withdrew the blade, the shooter paused and raised his hands in surrender. Not as eager to die as the rest, he dropped his handgun and ran for it, ditching Piatkowski. The shrouded stranger wasn't done though and retrieved the handgun from off the ground. They fired two shots, killing the last Russian from twenty yards out.

Piatkowski was just as stunned as I, both of us watching as they sheathed their sword, barely breathing from the effort. The random stranger turned toward me. I kept my gun leveled at them, figuring I might last two seconds at best. But they didn't attack me. Instead, they yanked off their hood, revealing to my surprise, a bronzish woman with dazzling, exotic eyes.

"Russians. I remember them in my land back when I was a child," she hissed, spitting on the dead bodies at her feet. "Thank you for allowing me this pleasure."

"Who?" I fumbled to begin, still unsure about dropping my guard.

She bowed ever so slightly at me. "A mutual friend said to keep an eye on you...for some reason," the slight woman remarked as she flashed the brand between her fingers. That damn Joseline. Even though she couldn't be here, she still had friends nearby. "I'll leave you to your business. Oh. There was a sniper up there," she said, in the past tense, as she pointed up and behind me.

I glanced at the towers where she'd just indicated, shuddering to think there had been a bullseye on me before she arrived...whenever that was. When I looked back, she was gone. But Piatkowski was still here, reminding me of it as he charged, knocking my nine from my hand. He worked me over good, first with body shots then punching me repeatedly in the face. I never took him for a boxer, but his jabs were effective. As I felt my eye swelling shut, I struggled to defend myself, but was at a two-to-one arm disadvantage. When he got cocky, I launched an off balance punch to his gut. He winced and doubled over as he backed off.

"You want to tell me your real name? '*Black Ghost*' doesn't work for me. I mean, since we're old friends and all," he coughed as he circled to get his wind back.

"Truth," I replied, equally out of breath and squinting at him. "My name is Truth."

"For real?" he responded as so many others did. "Your mom was a hippie or something? Maybe a Black Panther back in the day?"

"See. It doesn't matter. Not anymore. One or both of us ain't leaving," I uttered as I tried to pivot toward my gun on the blood-streaked grass.

Piatkowski saw what I was trying to do and kicked it further away.

"I knew Orlovsky almost killed you in Paris!" he cheered, motioning at my sling. "It was stupid to challenge me like this anyway, but with one arm? And here I thought you had some kind of brains. That little Afghan girl evened the odds some, but I'm still way better than you, cripple," he taunted, figuring he had the edge. I swung wildly and missed. He kicked me in the back, knocking me onto my face. He immediately winced, noticeably limping before righting himself.

"And you still slightly drag your right leg. Accident from when you were active CIA when the boys liked you? When they let you sit at their lunch table?" I clowned in retaliation.

"You mean before you took away my life? My career? My family?" he ranted like a madman as he kicked me repeatedly on the ground, ignoring the pain in his leg. As he violently stomped away, my body went numb.

"Cry me a river," I spat from a bloody mouth, laughing at my grim fate while further enraging him. He went in for the kill and jumped atop me, raining a flurry of punches and elbow strikes. As I tried to block them, he pinned my free arm beneath his knee. I attempted to squirm free and roll him off me, but Piatkowski gripped my throat and began choking me. With his fingers digging into my windpipe, he pulled out a blade from under his pant leg.

"You're beaten. You've always been a loser. Except now you finally realize it," he gloated as he raised his hand overhead. "This is for those years in that dungeon," he pledged. As the blade plunged toward my chest, I suddenly blocked it. His blade broke against my heavily wrapped forearm; the arm I wasn't supposed to be able to use.

Piatkowski was stunned, realizing the truth far too late for it to matter. He was beaten. He was a loser. And now he finally realized it.

I jabbed my armored arm into his throat then hit him with a backhand, knocking several teeth loose. He fell off me and tried to crawl away, coughing with words coming out as broken as his jaw. As I slowly rose to my feet, I found a holstered knife on the disemboweled Russian and claimed it. "Appear weak when you are strong," I quoted from Sun Tzu's *Art of War* as I planted a foot on Piatkowski's back. I gradually applied more and more pressure, relishing in his discomfort. I played the long game, feigning the severity of my arm injury the entire time, even to Joseline. I had to be convincing to bring out the hyenas.

"Fuckin' nigger," he gurgled as I grabbed him by his hair. For his racist mouth, I jabbed the blade once under his armpit just to wound him.

"You hear that? The music has stopped, Mr. Smith. Alas, our dance is over," I calmly stated in his ear as I pressed the blade to his throat.

A whirring sound in the sky above the twin cooling towers drew my attention. All I could make out was a shadow, but it was some kind of aircraft circling overhead.

"Don't move!" an authoritative voice yelled before I even knew we had company. There were about seven of them that had us surrounded, assault rifles drawn. They weren't South African, but certainly were military of some sort in all black but with no insignia.

"I don't know who you are, but this is none of your business," I assured them as I pressed the blade even harder against his throat, relishing the use of a hand I'd intentionally neglected these past few weeks.

"Sir, put down the knife. That man there is wanted by the United States government and we have orders to bring him in alive. So, I'm only going to ask you one more time before we take more extreme measures," the helmeted man in charge stressed, never lowering his rifle. The rest of them were stunned at the carnage left by Joseline's friend, carefully surveying for survivors in the grass. They'd find none, but probably assumed it was my doing. I looked up again, now recognizing the shadow circling overhead as a drone. It didn't take the U.S. long to realize one of their own had surfaced and decided to get involved.

Piatkowski leaned back, smirking at me through a mangled mouth. "I guess you lose," he murmured with a chuckle.

I assessed the situation as well as how much I'd invested in this moment right here. I wiggled my fingers on the blade as I deliberated with guns drawn on me. "I guess I do," I replied.

Just as I viciously slit Piatkowski's throat, the serrated blade ripping into his flesh as I exacted my revenge.

"No!" the one in charge yelled as I dropped the blade and stood up. As the soldiers swarmed us barking in unison, I watched Piatkowski flop around on the ground, desperately trying to stem the bleeding. But I'd cut too deep. Even for the medic with them.

They made me stay on my knees with my hands behind my back as they tried to save their rogue asset. But in the end, it was all for naught. I felt a weight lift off my chest, almost shedding a tear of joy as the medic shook his head. I grinned at their commander when he finally looked my way. "What now?" I asked, knowing they had no jurisdiction here and that their little mission was covert. Maybe I could somehow still talk my way out of this.

"What now? Well, we got the terrorist responsible for the Paris attacks, I reckon," he replied as he walked over and got in my face, his men still aiming at me. His breath smelled like wintergreen gum. Funny that I would be the one caught in a lie, Orlovsky's last laugh. "You bought yourself a one-way ticket to GITMO, boy. And you ain't ever coming out," he crowed.

Right before he hauled off and busted me in the head with the butt of his rifle.

41-Truth

Two Days Ago

Joseline slept soundly after our night of working the kinks out of one another. I gently closed the bedroom door, leaving her to her restful slumber. Away from prying eyes, I removed my arm from the sling and stretched it out. It was burned and severely bruised in the Paris explosion with maybe some ligament damage, but still functioned and not as bad as I pretended it to still be. But I would play the game until Piatkowski was gone from my life forever. Last night, I acted indifferent with Joseline about finding him, but my desire for vengeance burned hotter than ever.

To smoke him out, I needed help; and from an unlikely place.

I placed a call across the ocean to New Orleans, reaching a man by the name of Ezell Singleton. Why him? Well, because his direct number was easier to get than his employer's.

"Hello?" he answered in an abrupt tone, seeing the call was from a blocked number.

"You know who this is?" I asked, remembering the run-ins we'd had when Piatkowski first tried to force me to do his bidding.

"What the fuck you want, punkass mother fucka? I dare you to show yo face around here. We ain't scared of you," he barked, the raspiness in his voice irritating to my ears.

"Maybe you should be scared. Look, put your boss on the phone, bitch ass. I got business to discuss," I dismissed as I walked onto the patio, sliding the door behind me.

I could hear quarreling in the background; probably Ezell telling her to just hang up. But as imposing as he was, he didn't call a single shot.

"By this call, should I assume Nate is gone?" Veronica Lewis asked with no reservations. She was a tough one.

"Not yet. But I plan on doing my best," I cheerfully answered.

"Fuck you! Now you wanna call and taunt me?" she growled.

"No. I'm calling to propose a truce. My roots are New Orleans too and we know some of the same people. That's how I got Ezell's number. I wanna end any beef we may have," I stated.

"Let's see. My brother's dead and my family's ruined. So how you gonna squash our beef? By throwing yourself in front a bus?" she suggested.

"No," I replied. "By restoring your family's standing. I know how powerful y'all were when your brother Bricks was alive. And I also know your current status. So let me propose this. Give me two names and they're no longer in your way."

"What the fuck do you mean by that?"

"Exactly what it sounds like. I'm returning the Lewis family to power in New Orleans, but with you at the head. Unless you've become comfortable with your salon and the breadcrumbs they toss your way. I'll even smooth things over with your *friends* south of the border. Now...give me two names," I stressed.

"You really got that kinda reach, boy?" Veronica asked, actually considering my proposal to put her on top of the Gulf Coast dope game.

"Let's just say I got somebody who can deliver. All I ask is for two names."

"What do you want in return?"

"When I deliver, you will deliver. You'll convince your baby daddy that I mean you harm. Then you'll convince him one more time what needs to be done," I spun, getting her to do as I say. Words, words, words.

"You're gonna kill, Nate," she muttered, inevitability slamming into her.

"Yes...and you can't stop it. But if you help me end this now, you get something out of it. Do we have a deal?" I finished.

"...Yeah. Nate gets on my fuckin' nerves anyway," she sighed as she had me write down the names of two enemies of hers in exchange for her betrayal.

All that was left was for me was a final act of nastiness once Joseline awakened. I was gonna miss having her by my side, but it was time for her to get off this bus. For now, I just put my arm back in the sling and took a seat on the patio. Maybe I'd cook something for her.

Epilogue-One year later

Guantanamo Bay "GITMO", Cuba

"Stand up and step back. Both hands out," the military guard ordered. Just as they did every day I'd been here. Early on, I'd fuck with them for my amusement and they'd make me pay. Broken bones heal though. I'd worry about my mind, but I've lost it too many times to count and it always found its way home.

"You need some motivation? I said 'move', prisoner!" he yelled as the three-man detail edged closer toward the bars.

Scratching my full beard, I cut a scathing look their way, but complied like an obedient dog. Since they snagged me in Soweto, I'd been treated as a high level threat/enemy combatant due to the trumped-up charges in connection with Paris. I imagine the world slept better at night feeling a terrorist had been captured rather than the convoluted idea that a petty Russian thug was responsible for their discomfort.

Russia, of course, didn't mind either. So I accepted my punishment, being bound and chained twenty-four hours a day under constant surveillance and questioned relentlessly by those who had no clue about how the world really works. At first, I tried telling the truth about what happened in Paris and Orlovsky's involvement in it, but that went over as well as expected. I think I was pretty entertaining with the stories I made up later under duress and sleep deprivation.

Until one day, I felt it was time to check-out of their lovely hotel.

"I need to make a call," I told the guard inspecting my shackles while the other checked my jumpsuit for concealed items. It was almost lunch time and I tired of them spitting in my food.

"Boy, you ain't got rights here. Now shut up and behave before you get waterboarded again," the Marine instructed. Yes, waterboarding sucks.

"If you're not going to let me make a call, I need a priority message delivered through your commander up in his fancy office with the nice cigars," I urged straight-faced and speaking more than I had the entire past month.

"And who the fuck are you trying to get a message to? The President?" he joked for his boys with a hearty laugh.

"Actually...yes," I answered with a smile, locking eyes with him. "Your Commander-in-Chief owes me a favor from way back."

You see, people hire me for all sorts of mayhem-blackmail, revenge, sabotage, straight pettiness.

Even for Presidential elections.

Most of the time, I'm paid up front or upon completion of services. But sometimes...I wait.

Nothing like the ultimate "Get Out of Jail Free" card, I thought as the American soldiers begrudgingly released me hours later. Stepping out the gate and to my freedom, I ambled toward the checkpoints of Cuba proper and the nearby town of Caimanera. I was newly freed, hungry for some ajiaco and in need of a decent haircut. The Cuban government wouldn't know what to make of this or me, but I'd come up with something convincing. It's what I do.

My name is Truth and I live in a very cold world. Maybe you'll meet me one day. But pray that you don't.

Discussion Questions

1. Would you like to read further adventures of Truth?

2. Would you like to read further adventures of Joseline?

3. How did you feel when you realized Sophia died?

4. Do you think there's a chance Sophia is still alive?

5. Were you convinced of the severity of Truth's injury?

6. What did you think of the dynamic between Truth and Joseline?

7. What was your favorite scene?

8. Who did you feel was a more worthy villain? Orlovsky or Piatkowski/Mr. Smith?

9. Do you feel Truth is truly evil?

About the Author

Eric Pete is an award winning author, his works having reached the bestseller lists of *The Dallas Morning News, Essence, USA Today* and the *New York Times.*

He is a U.S. Army veteran and member of Delta Sigma Pi Professional Business Fraternity.

Born in Seattle, Eric developed a love for reading and late night movies at an early age. It wasn't until later in life that he finally gave in to the movies in his own head and began his journey as a writer.

A graduate of McNeese State University, he currently resides in Texas where he is working on his next project.

Made in the USA
Middletown, DE
03 May 2016